I0674797

Adventures
of Tarzan

"ADVENTURES
OF
TARZAN"

The Wild Animal Serial Supreme

STARRING

Elmo Lincoln

IN

15 Electrifying Episodes

PRODUCED BY
GREAT WESTERN PRODUCING CO.
For WEISS BROTHERS'
NUMA PICTURES CORP.

PICTURIZED FROM THE CONCLUDING CHAPTERS OF
"THE RETURN OF TARZAN"
By

Edgar Rice Burroughs

LIONS, ELEPHANTS, CROCODILES, LEOPARDS,
APES, MONKEYS AND A HOST OF OTHER JUNGLE
DENIZENS. SCENE AFTER SCENE OF THRILL AND
EXCITEMENT IN EACH EPISODE OF "ADVENTURES
OF TARZAN." THE HEROIC LINCOLN AS TARZAN,
THE APE-MAN, IS THE CENTRAL FIGURE IN A
SERIES OF HAIR-BREADTH ESCAPES AND WONDER-
FUL STUNTS WHICH WILL KEEP YOU ON THE EDGE OF
YOUR CHAIR THROUGHOUT THE ENTIRE SERIAL.

"THE TARZAN OF TARZANS"

Adventures of Tarzan

By

Maude Robinson Toombs

ERBville Press

First Edition

"Adventures of Tarzan" is based on the film version of the 15 chapter serial, "Adventures of Tarzan", written by Lillian Valentine and Robert F. Hill, which was based on the concluding chapters of "The Return of Tarzan" by Edgar Rice Burroughs. Except for minor spelling corrections, here, for the first time in book form, is reprinted the COMPLETE newspaper serialization as it originally appeared in the Sedalia Democrat newspaper in issues dated March 22-24, 26-31, and April 2-7, 1921.

Copyright 1921
Copyright not renewed

Published January 2006

ISBN 978-1-64720-678-9

Fiction House Press
www.FictionHousePress.com

TABLE OF CONTENTS

Adventures
of Tarzan

ADVENTURES OF TARZAN

CHAPTER I

JUNGLE ROMANCE

"**S**he's a goner!" the captain bawled above the shrieking of the wind. "All hands to the boats!"

As he spoke, the deck of the Lady Alice dipped sharply under his feet and a giant comber smothered the side rails in a mass of foam. It was plain the yacht was sinking by the minute and there would be hardly time to make the boats.

Rokoff the Nihilist sprang into the first one and vainly try to hold its sides steady against the solid wall of wind and rain that beat with tropical fury.

"Quick! Damn you!" he shouted to Earl of Greystoke, who was lowering his fiancee, Jane Porter, into the tipping, plunging craft.

The glare of lightning showed the pale face of the fourth member of the party—the aged scientist, Jane's father. He shook with fright as he clutched Greystoke's arm and tried to gather courage to step down into the treacherous blackness. At this moment the crippled yacht took a further downward plunge, Rokoff's hold was broken and the boat swung clear. With an oath Greystoke struck away the old man, and leaped straight for the half filled boat. He landed on the edge of it, and it all but capsized, as a huge wave first lifted and then sucked it down into its angry depths. Half drowned and unconscious, he was drawn aboard by Rokoff and Jane. When they turned in the direction of the Lady Alice it had vanished into the bowling wind and rain that made up the tropical night.

It was about four hours before dawn. In the darkness ahead lay the coast of Africa. Jane Porter, crouching in the bottom of the boat, prayed for the safety of her father. She had not seen Greystoke's cowardly action, she only feared the other life boat had also been swept away.

"If Tarzan were alive and here with us, he would have save daddy!" she sobbed to herself, filled with the memory of the man she loved, the King of the Jungle, who was so wonderful and so powerful, and who had given her up because he felt the handicap of having been mothered by a she ape, and brought up in the wild—and he wanted her be a great lady and to be happy. They had told her the sudden news of his death by drowning off the coast of Africa as he was about to return there on a mission for the French Secret Service. Jane thought of all these things in the hours when the tempest finally wore itself out, and the sky began to grow lighter.

Greystoke, who had been shaken to his senses by Rokoff and forced to help pull against the heavy waves, also must have been thinking of Tarzan.

"It was somewhere around these parts that we knocked him overboard," he whispered hoarsely to his companion. "D'ye think it could have been his ghost that almost did for us tonight?"

The Russian looked his contempt for the weaker man's superstition. "No—" he snarled—"sharks probably got him in these waters before he went far—and they didn't leave enough of him

2

to have a ghost!"

They both lowered their voices and glanced uneasily at the girl who lay face downward against the thwarts.

It was noticeable that, with the sinking of the yacht, the respect Rokoff had for its owner seemed to have disappeared also. When exhausted, and with their boat pounded to pieces by the breakers, they were finally thrown up like so much wreckage on the shore, it was Rokoff who came to his senses first, who took command of the party with an iron hand, and who began by separating the girl from Greystoke as they gained the shelter of an abandoned hut and sank more dead than alive on its bare floor to forget their misery to sleep.

But, in another part of the forest, only a short distance away, Tarzan, whom they thought dead, was very much alive. In his leafy couch high in the tree tops, he awoke to a dawn that tinged the white plumage of the cockatoos a delicate rose, that filled the jungle with the twitterings and the brightened colorings of approaching day.

The renewed wonder of it filled Tarzan with the old delight in just strength—in using it to defend those of his wild brothers who were weaker than he.

Already padded footsteps could be heard. Through the underbrush stealthy creeping forms set the bushes swaying. The jungle was awakening and prowling for its food. Above the ripple of the little spring which gushed from the rock near the base of his tree he could hear the whimpering of Naja, the mother ape, as she nursed her young. There was a sudden rush through the undergrowth and Tarzan peered downward through the branches just in time to see a spotted shape hurl itself straight for the little family. With a quick fling of his trusty rope he caught the snarling leopard in mid air, and he left it dangling helplessly by its middle, securely trussed, from the great limb of the tree.

Naja chattered her thanks. Tarzan threw out his chest, and, beating his hands against his sides gave vent to the terrible war cry of the apes, the call of triumph and of death.

As the dreadful sound rang through the forest even Numa, the lion, fled in fear, for he knew the King of the Jungle had returned. Leopard, puma and panther realized that death lurked for them at the end of Tarzan's trusty rope or his sharp flashing knife. Only Tantor, the elephant, and Tarzan's faithful ally, recognized the war cry with joy and trumpeted back his answering welcome.

Through the close undergrowth the tribe of apes began to gather to look over this stranger who used their language. During Tarzan's absence in England he had changed and shed his hair. The young bull apes of the clan, not knowing him, flung themselves on him savagely and he met them with fierce blows, after the manner of their kind. One great bull ape who tried to crush him in his long powerful arms was seized by Tarzan and thrown violently into the brambles.

Then the tribe, realizing the superior strength of the stranger, listened to Naja the she-ape as she told of his great bravery in saving her from the leopard. The older members gathered closer and looked more sharply at their former friend and leader. Suddenly great yells of the old bull apes rent the air and Tarzan sent his own voice ringing through the forest in the same cries. He had found his tribe, and they once more recognized him as their great friend and leader, after his two years absence.

In the other part of the woods where Rokoff, Greystoke and the girl were trying to find food and shelter there was also bitter strife. Rokoff insisted on rationing off strictly the few bananas they were able to gather—and he looked at the girl. She clung to the side of the man she expected to marry, but he, being more than half a coward, compared his own with the huge Russian and hesitated to take the offensive. Besides, he had the same interests with Rokoff—and Rokoff knew that he, William Clayton, had used his wealth to steal the title which really belonged to Tarzan, and to influence the girl by this means.

As if tired of temporizing, the Russian moved the slighter man toward the jungle.

"Leave us alone!" he ordered advancing toward Jane.

Clayton refused with an oath, and taking the girl by the arm he drew her to his side. "Give me the right to protect you from that swine Rokoff!" he whispered savagely.

"How can we be married according to the law away out here in the wilds!" Jane exclaimed, and then her fingers closed around the locket which Tarzan had given her: "Besides, William," she continued, "I have been thinking—and I have the queerest feeling that Tarzan is still alive and will come back to me."

He shrugged his shoulders. "Rokoff and Hazel Strong both told you—" he began, but was interrupted by the furious Rokoff.

Blinded by tears Jane fled into the little hut and crouched behind the doorway. She heard the men in violent discussion.

"Remember," Clayton answered to some taunt, "that you are as much responsible for the death of Tarzan as I am!"

"You instigated the death, I merely executed it!" cried Rokoff.

"I paid you twenty thousand pounds to put Tarzan out of the way. That clears my conscience!" sneered Clayton.

An ugly note was in Rokoff's voice. "My friend," he drawled, "in England you had the first claim on the girl. This is No Man's Land. Should we be rescued, you may make her Lady Greystoke—but—" he stroked his moustache, "while we're here—"

Jane crouched against the rough logwork of the cabin, pressed Tarzan's locket to her lips, and prayed for death.

Clayton's answer was to spring at his rival's throat. There was a short, sharp struggle and then the Russian allowed him to rise to his feet, dizzy and bleeding.

"And, now," purred he, "that you're ready to listen to reason, I'll let you in on a secret. Before throwing Tarzan overboard, being a wise man, I went through his pockets and took his private papers. That was a good thing my friend, for imagine what I found? No less than the secret formula of a deadly gas, the ingredients for which are controlled by his government. But, my dear Greystoke, as long as I hold their formula, their minerals are useless to them."

He took a piece of sheepskin from inside his shirt and held it over the fire, beckoning to Clayton to come and read it over his shoulder. Under the action of the heat a secret formula appeared traced with chemicals on the skin as follows:

> 5 Gr. N A-Cl.
> 5 Gr. H-"O
> 5 Gr. C. C. —H.C. L.

Rokoff's big frame was shaking with unpleasant laughter. "This means, my slow friend," he boasted, "that with this formula I hold the lives of any nation in the palm of my hand! And that you could receive millions should anything happen to me and should you present this to my chief."

The jug of water which Clayton was raising to his lips shook, and he spilled some of the fluid over Rokoff and the parchment.

"But never fear, my friend," the Russian finished slowly, "nothing will happen 'to me that does not happen to you also—so, is it not better that we split the proceeds and do not let a silly girl come between us?" His voice broke in the middle of his sentence as his eyes stared horror stricken at the parchment, where, under the action of water, new characters were appearing, written in synthetic ink by Tarzan:

> "In lower Egypt I find M. Rokoff and M. Gernot have planted the seeds of bolshevism against our government. I shall follow them to Egypt where Gernot plans a raid on slaves and ivory traders to cover his real purpose: that of securing the plans of our N. A. C. L. mine."

Rokoff ground his teeth. It was his death warrant that Tarzan had traced on the sheepskin, and he could not even destroy it because of the valuable formula also recorded there and which he had no means of copying. He replaced it inside his belt and vented his fury on the other man.

"Now, damn you, get out!" he blazed. "I'm in command here. Go to the lookout point — anywhere — but make yourself scarce!"

Clayton, realizing that he was the weaker, fled like the coward that he was, and Rokoff shouted to the terror stricken girl:

"Now you're mine as long as we are here!"

Her answer was to slam the door of the hut closed and to hold it so with her body. Rokoff hurled his full strength against it and it gave way, suddenly precipitating him into the center of the room. While he gathered himself to his feet Jane rushed out through the open doorway, preferring to trust herself to any danger outside rather than to this brute within.

The Russian started in hot pursuit and his cries brought Clayton also on the hunt. Both men were determined that she should not escape them.

She fled blindly through the thick underbrush. Her feet tripped over twisted roots and her dress caught in the briers and twice she fell. Close at hand she heard the roar of a lion and still she kept out hoping, by twisting and turning on her trail, to elude her pursuers, and if she did not, and fell into the lion's jaws instead, she felt it was infinitely preferable to having the two human beasts obtain possession of her again.

A wind blew straight from the sea past them and in the direction where Tarzan leaned in the crotch of a great moss grown tree. His keen nostrils caught the scent of both man and lion, and he swung lightly from branch to branch in their direction. He only paused long enough to set the panther he had snared with his rope free, as he passed the bough where he had left the now thoroughly cowed animal swinging. Tarzan was merciful and, realizing that a hungry lion was near, he wished to give the smaller beast a chance for its life.

Again thunder of the lion's roar made everything tremble in the jungle. It was much nearer and Tarzan heard the crashing of the branches at the same time as the girl fled her pursuers. And at last he saw her, panting and sobbing for breath, trip over a moss grown limb which was half concealed under a mass of brilliant forest creepers. At the same time that she fell exhausted, there was the spring of a long yellow body and Numa, the lion, sure of his prey now, landed full upon her.

Tarzan gave two mighty swings downward aided by the tough vines which hung from the trees, and flung his powerful hands at the lion's throat. There was a short sharp struggle then, laughing aloud at his own strength, he choked Numa helpless and stabbed him to the heart.

The girl lay half conscious on the bank. Tarzan never noticed her as he threw back his head and, beating on his chest triumphantly, gave his mighty bull ape cry of victory. Behind him Rokoff and Clayton had crept upon Jane, but, even as they started to drag her away, they trembled with fright and exclaimed to each other:

"That man was Tarzan!" And Rokoff added, "We must fight side by side now or he'll get us!"

Jane, struggling out of her unconsciousness, heard the beloved name and glimpsed the muscular back and broad shoulders of the giant she loved and thought dead and her call echoed through the forest:

"Tarzan—OH, TARZAN!"

Clayton's hand went over her mouth, but too late. With a terrible cry Tarzan turned and saw her struggling in their arms. He sent them flying stunned and bleeding into the rocks and brambles and gathered her to his heart.

"Jane!" his voice broke on the word. "Oh, Jane—!" All the love and the longing in the world were in his voice. She lay against him, not saying a word, and presently he drew her away and looked into her eyes.

"And that man—are you his wife?" he asked.

She shook her head. "No, we are not married yet, and now I know we never shall be. I would rather trust myself out here with the beasts of the jungle than with him!"

"I have found worse things in what men call civilization than here," answered Tarzan gravely.

Neither of them noticed that Rokoff and Clayton had stolen quietly away, without a sound. They crawled to the summit of a great rocky knoll where they halted to examine their injuries. A series of snarls and muffled roars almost at their feet made them hold their breath in terror. Rokoff was the first to discover a trap in which a full grown lioness was trying to bite her way through the tough wooden bars. There was a sliding door which worked to open and close the trap by means of a rope. Rokoff looked toward Clayton and both men exchanged an ugly smile. Directly in the animal's path as he leapt to freedom would be Tarzan and the girl below.

Hiding behind the wooden cage they pulled on the rope which released the trap door. The lioness sprang out and stood one moment silhouetted against the sky as Jane's horrified eyes saw her.

"Tarzan—oh, Tarzan, LOOK OUT!" she screamed.

There was an answering roar from the opposite cliff, as another lion bounded forward, and without the slightest warning, both animals sprang downward and bore Tarzan to the earth.

CHAPTER II

THE CITY OF GOLD

When the two lionesses sprang down upon Tarzan he had already drawn his long knife and the larger of the two leaped directly upon the point and was almost ripped open from throat to hindquarters. Tarzan closed in a struggle with the other and cracked its ribs in a mighty embrace, as he found its heart and stabbed it through and through. Rokoff and Clayton, who had watched him from above, felt their knees tremble under them as they saw the giant toss to one side the limp carcass of the second lion and as they heard once more ringing in their ears his mighty cry of victory which drove every living thing to cover.

"For God's sake, let's get out of here!" Clayton begged. "Let's head south and cut our way through the deep forest rather than face that madman who is half a wild animal himself."

Rokoff, who had grown rather white around the mouth, agreed with him and the two conspirators fled through the underbrush, never stopping to look to the right or left.

But without their knowing it another danger was menacing them. From the south through the green forest a curious little band of dwarfs wound its way. With strange chants and gutteral cries, and leaps and bounds they followed a huge black ape which apparently led them. And the ape could only be distinguished in the slightest degree from the dwarfs in sheer brute ugliness.

These were the men of Opar, a race that lived in an underground city and worshipped the sun. Just now their omens had decreed that they must find some human sacrifices. The Sun god was angry and made his displeasure felt by the rumblings and flames of the volcano which almost directly overhung their cave city. The sacred bull ape of the Temple had been taught much of their language by the queen, La, and she had ordered him to lead them on to find fresh victims.

Rokoff was the first to notice the faint beating of the tom toms, which, at first almost imperceptible, grew in volume until it set everything a quiver in the forest. He climbed into a tree and what he saw of the savage men and their painted faces and whirling knives and clubs sent him flying deeper into the underbrush, saving his own self as usual and leaving Clayton to his fate.

But luck was still against him. He lost his bearings, tore around in a circle and ran straight into the arms of the huge bull ape, who had scented him and led the tribe in his direction. Rokoff was a strong man, a brute in every way and he put up a stiff fight, but he was no match for the swarm of little men who soon had him stunned with their clubs and bound hand and foot with the tough strands of creepers which hung from the trees. Having trussed him securely, they slung him from a pole and the bull ape, who scented more white flesh, led them on.

Meantime Clayton was hopelessly lost in the jungle, and, as he floundered among the rank high grass, which filled him with a mad horror of snakes and poisonous reptiles, he heard the trumpeting of an elephant and saw the trees bending and swaying as a huge body pressed its

13

way past them. It was Tantor, but not the gentle Tantor that Tarzan knew. Now he was an animal whose little pig eyes gleamed like fire, whose trunk curled upward, and whose huge ears flapped in anger. The big elephant did not tolerate strangers in his part of the forest. He charged in the direction of Clayton, who, tangled in the wild vines, made poor progress as he turned and ran for his life. It was easy work for Tantor to catch him.

"R-r-rum-p-h-h!"

It was half a squeal of rage, half a peevish cough, that Tantor gave as he wound his huge trunk around the trembling Clayton and threw him high up into the air. He then trumpeted shrilly and would no doubt have followed his victim to trample him with its broad feet, but his call of triumph was answered by another cry in the distance, and, recognizing the voice of his friend, Tarzan of the Apes, Tantor hurried forward to find what trouble he was in.

This is what had happened. The wind blowing in Tarzan's nostrils had warned him of the approach of the strange bull ape and of the pygmies.

"Go into the cabin dear," he ordered Jane, as he pushed her gently in the direction of the little lean-to he had built and she hardly had the time to obey his directions before the bull ape was upon him.

Naja, the she-ape, watched the battle from the limb of a tree where she had her home with her little one. She chattered back and forth on the branch as the contestants rolled over and over, giving shrill cries and gutteral sounds in which the man took part as well as the beast. Tarzan had been a former playmate of Naja's and

14

her heart was full of gratitude toward him for saving her little one from the leopard—but there was nothing she could do to help him this time. Her friend and the bull ape were locked in such a tight embrace that to have interfered might have been dangerous. Finally Tarzan managed to get the ape on its back and was raising his sharp blade when the dwarfs came to the rescue and beat him unconscious with their bludgeons. Then leaving him for dead, they burst into the cabin and dragged the fainting girl away with them. They now had all the human sacrifices they needed.

When she was quite sure that they had gone Naja swung down from her branch and went to the help of the unconscious Tarzan. She raised his head tenderly, much as a human being might have done, brought him water in a piece of gourd and restored him to consciousness by licking his wounds.

Tarzan sat up dazed and bleeding. In his whirling brain there was the premonition of a great evil. He looked dizzily around and, seeing the cabin door wide open and Jane gone, he knew that something dreadful had happened. Then Naja, still holding him in her hairy arms, told him in ape language that the little brown tarmangani had stolen his sweetheart and that the big mangani was still able to lead them.

Tarmangani in monkey language means men, and a mangani is an ape.

It was just at this moment that Tarzan heard the trumpeting of Tantor. Half mad with rage and sorrow he answered it with his own cry, and the big elephant came plunging through the forest toward him, never caring for the young trees which he uprooted from his path in his haste.

Into the big sail-like ears Tarzan poured his black trouble and the friendly trunk, now grown gentle, curled around his waist and swung him on the broad back. The two comrades set off as fast as they could in the direction Naja pointed out to them, where the men of Opar had disappeared with Jane.

Meanwhile, away where Tantor had left him, Clayton had fallen through the bushes into quicksands and was struggling with a badly strained back to pull himself out. But the harder he tried, the further he sank in, until the treacherous sands rose like water to his arm pits. In his despair he let out scream after scream so that the monkeys fled chattering through the branches, and the birds whirred in wild alarm from their nests—so that every living thing avoided the spot save one big vulture who appeared lazily sailing and circling directly above him, as if well content to bide his time which he knew would be short. And seeing that evil shadow between him and the sun, the false Earl of Greystoke gave one last cry of despair.

At the sound, an old man in ragged khaki stopped looking for a brilliant hued insect which had escaped him, and ran to the edge of the quicksands where Clayton was struggling. At the sight of him, the imprisoned man thought he was having delirium or was already judged and condemned, for the face he saw before him was that of Jane's father whom he had knocked down on the night of the wreck and left to drown. But it was not the professor's ghost. He had been saved after all with the rest of the English party in the second boat and, as he seized Clayton's outstretched hands and held him from sinking deeper, he exclaimed anxiously:

"Where is my daughter?" All he remembered was the child he loved so dearly.

"In — the — jungle — with Tarzan," Clayton gasped, then: "For God's sake, save me!" he shrieked, as the professor involuntarily relaxed his hold and he felt himself once more sucked downward.

The old man was nearly dragged in with him and saved himself with difficulty by seizing hold of a bush nearby. Then followed an unequal struggle in which Jane's father exerted every ounce of strength he possessed and for every inch he drew Clayton out, when he relaxed, the sand pulled him down two more. The older man's failing strength might have caused him also to fall a victim if a diversion had not occurred. Frightened by something behind them, three great lions bounded across the open space. They came straight for the professor who, in his terror, wrenched himself free and ran for his life. When he recovered his breath he tried to do his duty and to find his way back, he was utterly lost and could not do so. Everything had grown ominously calm in the jungle, only another big black vulture had joined its mate and was lazily circling in the sunlight.

At the very moment his daughter and Rokoff were being brought as captives before Queen La in the subterranean temple of the sun in the hidden city of Opar.

La was a tall woman, almost white, with tawny hair and large yellow eyes like a lion's. She was like a lioness in disposition too, she was treacherous and feline, fearing no man and loving few for long. Just now her favorite was David, her chief warrior, because he was taller than the rest of her subjects and had made more conquests in battle, so she appointed him to be the high priest, and for the time being, he enjoyed her smiles.

La was barbarically dressed in a spotted bull's hide and wore many anklets and bracelets of beaten gold around her ankles and her shapely arms. Jane ran toward her with outstretched arms, hoping for pity, but the cruel hearted La thrust her aside so violently that she tore the covering from Jane's slender shoulders.

The queen's subjects had laid before her nuggets of virgin gold chiseled from the hillside and bars of the precious metal lay in piles which caused Rokoff's eyes to light up with covetousness. Outside the roar of a lion was heard and a big, ugly black-maned head was seen against the grating which let in light and air.

David, the high priest, waved his hand with what he believed was a graceful gesture. "Your treasure is well guarded from without, O queen," he ventured. "None dare venture where Numa watches!"

But La yawned behind her bracelets. David bored her with his gentle ways. She was already very tired of him.

Realizing that he was making a poor impression, the favorite directed her mind to another subject. "Good tidings, O Queen," he exclaimed bowing low, "Your warriors have returned with strange white sacrifices for your gentle hands."

La's red lips curled scornfully. "Only this girl—" she began, and then her eyes fell on Rokoff, who was being brought forward from the rear. Always a coward at heart, he decided that it would be good to live and enjoy some of the gold which almost blinded him as it lay piled up against the sides of the room. He looked insolently at her out of his bold blue eyes. After all, savage though she was, she was a woman and he was a man.

La felt the rough power of the stranger with the ruddy face and the eyes like blue fire. Her bosom rose and fell, she swayed toward him like the child of nature that she was—then before the swift angry features of David her eyes fell and a little grim smile curved her lips. This prisoner would not be sacrificed just yet anyhow— she would find out whether he could please her first. As for David, there were ways of getting rid of Davids when their usefulness was ended. The stranger might take the high priest's place very nicely—and he certainly looked very big and handsome. She gazed at Rokoff's coarse face long and deeply.

"Sacrifice the girl," she ordered coldly. "See, our master, the Sun, has veiled his face with smoke from the angry mountain (she meant the volcano) and he must be appeased with human blood."

The men of Opar circled around Jane with cries and wild yells. Every now and then they would stop, and bowing their heads to the ground, they would chant their invocations that their Lord the Sun might pour on them once more his golden smile and that the angry mountain might be stilled. Then two of the men seized the girl and placed her, throat upwards, on the sacrificial stone.

La mounted the altar steps beside her and snatching a richly jewelled knife from the golden belt, she held it high above the breast of the terror-stricken girl.

"Oh Lord of the Sun, prepare to receive our

19

atonement," La chanted, and the dwarfs after repeated in their gutteral accents "—our atonement."

"Oh, Tarzan, this is good-bye forever," thought poor Jane, little dreaming that at this very moment her lover had alighted from Tantor's back at the foot of the rocky hillside almost devoid of vegetation which covered the hidden city of Opar, and was making his way painfully over the rough stony incline seeking a crevice through which he could find out where she was.

The volcano above was rumbling wickedly and every now and then heaving out showers of small redhot stones which Tarzan had to dodge and which made his progress all the harder. Finally he reached a spot which he remembered on his previous journeys and, looking through the narrow aperture in the solid rock, saw to his horror, his sweetheart laid on the altar, and the vengeful La poised above her with the sacrificial knife upraised in her jewelled hands.

To think was quick with Tarzan, to act was quicker. Only by such swiftness do beasts and men survive in the jungle. He heaved and tore at a great rock until he lifted it with his massive shoulders, then with a well directed twist he sent it spinning down through the opening straight into the middle of the circle of dancers.

The chant stopped instantly and the tom toms ceased in the middle of a beat. There arose a cry of terror:

"The volcano!"

The dancers huddled together. The queen hastily left the altar and joined them. Rokoff hastily seized this opportunity to creep back to where Jane lay bound. Desire for her still held him in its spell. He did not know whether she was unconscious, but bent close to her ear and whispered:

"You are too beautiful to be sacrificed. I'll try to save you!" At this moment the queen and the men of Opar missed him and angrily snatched him from the girl's side. David's lips twisted into a smile as he noticed the jealous look the queen gave Rokoff; he faced the tribe and shouted:

"Sacrifice both the man and the girl, so shall the wrath of the Sun be averted."

"Ah-h-h-h!" the crowd screamed its approval—the tom toms began to beat again—the squat forms to circle. Rokoff felt himself seized from behind and pushed toward the rock of sacrifice.

"Stop!" It was La who spoke haughtily. This infringement of authority had decided her. The blue eyed stranger should live. After all, once the girl was killed he would forget her. "No, I am still the queen," she cried, "and the girl and not the man shall be sacrificed."

Once more she raised the knife of sacrifice on high—once more the chants began.

The volcano rumbled menacingly, a cloud of sulphur and acrid smoke almost blinded and choked Tarzan as he exerted all his strength once more and heaved on his mighty shoulders another boulder which he sent crashing after the first.

This time the chants ended with screams from those warriors caught by the rock. Then, as Tarzan sprang to look through the crevice once more, there was a hiss and a roar as of some monster, a shower of stones and pieces of large rock, and the whole mountainside seemed to groan and convulse itself in agony. With a report which could have been heard for miles, the solid rock split in two right under Tarzan's feet, hurling

21

him downward through clouds of steam and lava.

CHAPTER III

THE SUN DEATH

At the convulsion of the volcano split open the solid rock, Tarzan felt as if he were falling downward into the very bowels of the earth. But, as a matter of fact, the earthquake was a slight one, and he landed no further than in the tunnels leading to the treasure chamber of Opar.

Stunned and bleeding, he lay on the hard floor amid a shower of rocks, and it was a few minutes before he was able to realize where he was and could pull himself together. Then he heard the chanting supplications of the dwarfs and realized, from his previous knowledge of the place, that he was near the chamber of sacrifice.

At the first sound of the shock, the queen and her warriors had fled out on the terrace beyond the temple of the sun. Rokoff seized this opportunity to hasten back to where Jane lay bound on the altar, more frightened far by the earthquake than she had been even by the bloodthirsty La. He seized her in his arms, ran across the altar through the doorway and into what proved to be the main treasure chamber. There he laid Jane in a pile of gold bars and, while his eyes traveled over the treasure which lined the walls and lay on the floor in glittering heaps, he made up his mind to have both the girl and the wealth of Opar.

"Come now, don't be a fool!" he entreated her roughly. "How can you get out of here without me? I have saved you once, I shall save you again—just love me as I ask you and all shall be well. I am going to capture some of this gold and there are millions that are going to be mine when I get back to civilization," he boasted. "What can you do, living here with a man monkey in the jungle? I can save you for myself, give you everything women like the most, everything that money can buy, and you'll share all my wealth with me and be a queen in your own right if you'll only listen to me."

But Jane only wept and shrank away from him as far as her bonds would allow.

"Tarzan—oh, Tarzan," she prayed inwardly, with all her soul and all her longing. "Come to me—I know you will! Save me!"

With a growl of disgust Rokoff pushed her from him. He was furiously angry and wished he might hurt and humiliate her. Suddenly an ugly smile lit up his face. He wanted a plan of the treasure chamber so he might come back and steal the gold—he had no paper, no ink, no parchment even—why could not her delicate skin serve him as the parchment on which he might draw the map that would give him at least one thing he desired, money?

Taking the pin in his belt buckle, he commenced to sharpen it against a piece of stone. Jane watched him with terrified eyes and tried to roll further away from him, but that was impossible because of the tightness of her bonds. When he decided the metal point had just the right jagged sharpness, he seized and pulled away with his great paw the covering over her right shoulder. Then, bearing down on the point with no idea of saving her, he slowly and carefully drew in the blood of her tender skin the plan of the treasure chamber of Opar.

"So you see, my dear," he remarked when he had finished, "at least you shall be useful to me and carry on your back the map of this place until I can copy it in better material."

Meanwhile, as there were no more earthquake shocks, Queen La and her warriors returned to the temple of the Sun only to find their victim gone, as well as Rokoff. The queen was about to order a search when into the doorway back of the altar loomed the great form of Tarzan.

Now Tarzan and the queen had met before he went away on his journey to England and she had fallen madly in love with him; in fact her passion had grown all the greater because he would have none of her. At the sight of the man she had repeatedly declared her love for, La forgot all but the fact that he had returned.

She was overjoyed and ran to meet him with outstretched hands. David— Rokoff even—became as nothing to her. She clung to him exclaiming:

"Ah, you have come back, wonderful tarmangani! Why did you run from me? Do you not realize that I can give you the untold fortunes of Opar and make you my king?"

But Tarzan, snatching her arms away, looked down upon her with eyes like cold stone. "What have you done with the girl your warriors brought here from the jungle?" he demanded.

"Why trouble yourself about the puny stranger when I am near?" purred La, letting her tawny hair brush his cheek as she bent close to his face. Her golden anklets tinkled musically, her large eyes glowed with a golden light. She seemed like some gorgeous and repulsive idol to Tarzan. He pushed away her arms, which crept and clung to his.

"Where is the girl?" he demanded again, and this time his voice was loud with a rising note of anger.

And La knew her powers of fascination were wasted on this giant.

"You give your thoughts to that little weakling when you might have my love!" she cried haughtily. Even now it is too late, for the Sun God has claimed her in sacrifice and she is no more, as you can see for yourself," and she pointed to the empty altar.

With a cry of rage which re-echoed through the vaults of Opar, Tarzan the man vanished and Tarzan of the Apes took his savage place. Before his bared teeth, before the fury of his red eyes even La quailed.

"You lie!" he cried. "You lie! And if you do not, the vengeance of all the jungle will fall on you and there will not be so much left of Opar that men may know it ever existed, and your bones will bleach on the spot where it was!"

The high priest David and the rest of the tribe gathered angrily around him as he thus defied their queen. David in particular a prey to his jealousy cried out:

"Enough! This bold stranger has defied both the queen and us — the punishment is death. Let us sacrifice him to the Sun God!"

"Death!" chanted the tribe.

"Let him die without delay," commanded the high priest, and in spite of La's pleadings, the warriors made a rush and overpowered Tarzan, beating him senseless with their bludgeons and binding him with ropes. The sacred bull ape, when he thought the big man secure, even attempted to fling himself on him in revenge for

26

the injuries he had received in the forest, but Tarzan kicked him right down the stone altar steps into the midst of the group of pygmies and the ape fled howling.

They tightened the ropes around his ankles more securely and laid him on the sacrificial stone. There he lay helpless while the chants once more arose and the queen was forced to raise the shining knife over his body. But the knife was slow to descend. La was fighting a losing fight—but it was a fight—with the gentler side of her nature. She knew that she must go on with the sacrifice if she still wished to be Queen of Opar, for David had the tribe with him, and there was a cruel light in his eyes.

"Why did I not get rid of this high priest before? Soon he will be king!" she thought, as the knife poised for its downward flight.

At that moment a girl's agonized cry sounded through the cavern:

"Tarzan! Oh, Tarzan!"

It was the voice of Jane, and it ceased suddenly because of the hand of Rokoff which smothered it. She was fighting for her life against him, determined to die a thousand times on the altar of the Sun God rather than allow this man to touch her. And then she heard the chant of the pygmies as the queen raised the knife and she immediately thought that perhaps Tarzan had followed her and had himself been seized and laid on the altar, for this was the song of sacrifice. And so with all her strength she called the name of the man she loved.

At the sound, a wave of fierce power swept over Tarzan. With a superhuman effort he swelled his great muscles and his bonds snapped. He staggered to his feet before the amazed eyes of

La, then as the pygmies started to overpower him, he seized a length of the rope lariatwise and sent it whistling over the body of the nearest to him. Then when the rope became taut, he swung his victim as a human sling to keep the others off.

With this flying human mass to protect him Tarzan backed away, scattering the men of Opar in wild terror. Still swinging the man as a protection he stepped backward across the altar and vanished through the doorway which led to the treasure room. There he found Rokoff struggling with Jane, and dropping his more dead than alive human freight, he sprang for the Russian's throat. Then followed a fight like that between wild beasts, while the girl cowered against the wall.

Tarzan beat down Rokoff's fists as one would slap down the hands of a child. Then he slammed him against the sides of the treasure vault, sent him crashing to the floor again and again and finally landed a smashing blow on his jaw which would have killed a less rugged man but which left Rokoff unconscious. Then Tarzan felt through his pockets to find the precious papers which had been taken from him. Under the Russian's belt he found the sheepskin parchment of the formula. He raised his voice in a great yell of victory and beat his palms against his chest.

At the sound Jane rushed to him, and he gathered her tenderly in his arms, cutting the bonds which still remained, and chafing her little wrists which were raw from the tight rope. But they did not have long in which to find comfort. Shouts and the sound of running feet showed that the pygmies had recognized the direction where Tarzan was hidden, by his yell of victory. They now rushed into the room, led by the jealous and infuriated La.

Tarzan lifted Jane up into a high opening which led into the outer world. "Run down the mountainside, dear," he told her. "I'll follow as soon as I can and I'll hold this entrance as long as possible to give you a good start."

With one backward glance through her tear-filled eyes, Jane fled through the high opening in the rock which led out on the steep side of the mountain. Stumbling, slipping and sliding, she tried to reach the place where Tarzan had told her Tantor waited, while back in the cave Tarzan placed himself on guard and prepared to hold his position against all comers.

The first onrush of the men of Opar was fatal to several of their number whom he met with flying fists and a cool eye. The pygmies retreated and seemed to be working up their courage for another advance. In this way they were encouraged by La, who, owing to her jealousy, had completely turned against Tarzan.

So intent were both parties that no one noticed Rokoff returning to consciousness and stealthily reaching out for one of the long bars of gold which were piled up at intervals along the sides of the treasure vault. With an effort he raised it up in both hands and brought it crashing upon Tarzan's head. Struck without the slightest warning from the rear, he went down in a heap and the pygmies flung themselves with cries of joy upon their enemy and joyously bore him to the altar of sacrifice. As they did so the Russian with a swift movement recovered the parchment formula.

La, the fickle, glided with her snakelike tread until she stood very close to Rokoff. Placing both hands on his shoulders she looked down into his eyes and spoke in honeyed accents.

"My brave warrior! La, the queen will reward you! What is your wish?"

"Only that the great queen will be pleased to smile on her captive." The lying Rokoff kept his eyes fixed on the ground lest she read the thought in them, which was that once she ceased watching him, he would make a very quick escape and only come back with some stout men at his back, not for her kisses but to rob her of liberty and treasure.

But David, the high priest, raged once more with jealousy as he saw the look that La gave the blue-eyed stranger as they both followed the tribesmen who bore the unconscious Tarzan into the temple of the Sun God. There they placed him on the altar stone and, seeing that he knew nothing of what was going on, Rokoff's cruel nature feared he would not suffer enough. Besides he knew that La possessed a nature similar to his own and that he could appeal to her in that way.

"Oh, great queen, I have a plan," he suggested.

She nodded her consent. Already this man was ruling her as David had done.

Rokoff went on. "Let me hold a shield of metal so that the sun's rays, as they come through this cleft in the rock, may be reflected on his unprotected body a million times more scorchingly than fire and add to his torments."

La clapped her hands to show her pleasure—anything cruel pleased her, particularly when her pride had been insulted.

Rokoff searched the place for something which might serve his purpose. The people of Opar did not seem to use any humbler metals than the living gold they dug from their own hillsides. His greed increased, if possible, as he realized the wonder of this. A large disc of the precious metal attracted his attention on account of its polished surface, and, holding this in such a manner that the sun's rays were levelled on the body of Tarzan, he waited patiently for the heat to rise in little swirls from his blistering flesh, which was only protected around his middle by a single leopard's skin.

The tropic sun played all over the captive with a most intense heat, but his torturer did not take into consideration the fact that the sun was the only doctor Tarzan had ever known in all the years that he lived among the apes. What would have burned another man severely only warmed and revived him like a beneficent healing hand. He became by degrees fully conscious but decided to lie there with his eyes closed and bide his time.

All of a sudden there was a cry of alarm from the pygmies. La and Rokoff, who stood with their backs to the rear doorway watching the sun begin to burn Tarzan, turned instinctively to look behind them. In the doorway stood what must surely have been the king of lions, and behind him, their jaws a drip and their eyes glaring, crouched three or four more of the lion pack. With a cry of terror La fled down the altar steps dragging Rokoff with her, and indeed he needed no urging to follow the rest of the pygmies.

At the screams and the running feet Tarzan raised his head slightly and opened his eyes, only to look straight into the yawning jaws of the biggest lion he had ever seen.

CHAPTER IV

STALKING DEATH

Quicker than a flash, Tarzan dropped back with closed eyes, and lay perfectly motionless while the lions, thinking him dead, raced right over him and leaped down on the other side of the altar in hot pursuit of La and the pygmies.

Tarzan opened his eyes cautiously. He was alone in the temple and the way of escape was clear. At this moment the voice of Jane, whom he thought safe and out of the vaults, rang through the air in a scream. She was in danger! It only took him about one second to clear the altar and to come running down the tunnel to where the sound came from, the treasure chamber.

Poor Jane had been forced to run back there to escape from a band of fierce lions, one of them had squeezed itself through the cleft in the rocks, and when Tarzan came in she was clinging desperately to a rope which hung from the ceiling while the hungry beast sat on his haunches waiting for her strength to fail so she would drop into his jaws. Every now and then he would snarl and strike out at her with a vicious paw, and then Jane in terror would slide a few inches further down the rope and have to regain with cut and bleeding fingers what she had lost of safety.

Uttering the terrible war cry of the apes, Tarzan fell upon the lion and soon had the animal severely wounded and put to flight. Then Jane fell into his arms half dead with exhaustion and so hysterical that he could hardly calm her. She sobbed and laughed by turns, her cheeks were red and burning, her eyes glassy, she seemed much more than frightened, she seemed as if she had a high fever. Jane's condition prevented Tarzan from avenging himself further on Rokoff as he would dearly have liked to do. The only sensible thing to do was to get the girl out of danger as soon as possible.

He picked her up in his arms as tenderly as if she had been a little child and carried her out on the rocky hillside to safety. They went in this way some distance, but, just as they were gathering courage from the fact that they heard no shouts and cries and that no one seemed to be following them, Tarzan laid his hand on her arm for silence as he stopped both to snuff the breeze and listen. Although even his keen ears could detect nothing, there was borne to him sharply and warningly the peculiar odor of the bull ape who acted as guide to the tribe of Opar. They were being followed then, and by this creature. A little cave was near by. Tarzan carried Jane into it, and crouched by her side waiting for the ape to catch up with them.

It was quite true that the ape was following. Queen La had heard Tarzan's cry of victory when he charged the lion which was attacking Jane and she knew he had escaped. She could do nothing about it at the time as both she and Rokoff were running from the lions, but just as soon as they had outdistanced them, and the lions had gone away after killing and dragging off several of the pygmies she went to find the ape and bade him follow Tarzan with his superior speed and agility and capture or even kill them.

At this Rokoff began to think. If he could

accompany their hairy guide he ran a good chance of escaping himself. He might even, if they followed Tarzan very far, be brought back to civilization by this means. It was worth taking a chance for. But he must approach the queen cautiously for it was very apparent that he had made a strong impression on her fickle fancy and that she would never let him leave her if she saw that was his intention.

He began by raising her hand to his lips and kissing it as he would that of a great lady. La, who was unused naturally to this form of endearment, nevertheless was touched by it as a more civilized woman might be and looked at him with softening eyes.

"Oh, La," began Rokoff, "in my country men would die for you and your slightest wish would be obeyed. You have made a slave of me with the wonder of your eyes. Let me do something for you which will prove my valor—let me show you that I also am brave. Let me bring to you the head of this girl, and this man bound as a captive."

The glitter of revenge came into the queen's eyes. "You are wise to prefer me to her," she caressed her bracelets of gold and lifted her tawny eyes which now burned into his. "I am La the golden—I am fair not as this puny child, but as a queen should be. I am not only a golden queen, I am a queen of gold and you shall share my treasure and my kingdom with me if you serve me well."

"Yes—I'll get the gold—to the devil with you, you savage! Just wait until I reach Gernot and his Arabs. Oh, if I only knew my bearings! They can't be very far from here—if that accursed yacht had not struck that reef just as we were so near our destination!" These thoughts traveled busily through Rokoff's treacherous brain, even as he held the queen's hand in his and lowered his head that she might not read the deceit in his eyes.

But La was after all but a simple savage, a child of nature. She threw herself into his arms and pressed into his hand one of her royal bracelets.

"Go, my brave warrior," she cried. "Go and win me revenge on the tarmangani and his mate who have defiled me. But do not stay long. La will be waiting the return of her king."

The ape was already bounding ahead. Rokoff seized a spear and with difficulty followed his quick pace. He was indeed quite a little behind and that is why Tarzan distinguished the ape's presence first.

To reach the cave Tarzan had put his pursuers off the trail by walking in the bed of a mountain stream, still carrying Jane, also Rokoff kept urging the ape to push on further that he might gain his own ends. It was therefore not surprising that Tarzan and the girl peering through the entrance of the cave, saw them trying to find footprints far below in the valley and finally disappear altogether in the direction of the north.

It was time they eluded their pursuers however for Jane's condition was becoming serious. She had periods when she babbled without sense or meaning, her rapidly rising fever had reached the danger point while her flushed cheeks and glassy eyes filled Tarzan's heart with worry. He realized that her condition was serious, although he did not know to what he could ascribe it.

Finally Jane, who was moaning and tossing, clutched at her shoulder and Tarzan laid his hand upon it, whereupon she cried out in pain.

35

Tenderly and with the utmost care he removed the ragged sleeve and then he saw the angry and inflamed series of cuts and scratches which made up the map of the treasure chamber of Opar.

"Who has done this to you?" His voice was so terrible that Jane drifted out of the haze of fever and answered him.

"Rokoff"—she gasped, "it burns like fire—he must have poisoned it—he did it with the pin of his—belt buckle—" her voice trailed off into weakness.

Tarzan clenched his fists until the great muscles stood out on his arms like cords. His face was not good to look upon.

"The beast—he'll pay for this," but he spoke aloud more to himself than to her. "I do not think he could have had time to poison it—or the materials in his possession—and then he would have wanted to preserve the map on a living person. It must be that the belt buckle was rusty or unclean and that it infected the shoulder. If I can lower this fever and get some herbs to put on the wound all will be well."

To Jane he said: "Courage, my dearest, I must carry you out of this down into the jungle where I will be able to care for you better and we must find some herbs which grow at the side of the river."

Then followed a perilous trip down the rest of the mountain with the girl a dead weight in his arms, finally they reached the plain and rested a moment in a meadow which was thickly covered with brilliant flowers and creepers that began to grow at the edge of the jungle.

The sun was very near going down, and Tarzan knew that he must not dream of trying to reach his tribe or his lair that night. The girl would never be able to stand the journey. The river was nearer and by the banks were certain bulbs and herbs with almost magic powers of healing—but every moment counted. If only Tantor were near by—the usually faithful animal had wandered away finding the wait too long and Tarzan did not dare to give the call for his four-footed brother to help him for this might bring enemies as well as friend upon them. Bara the deer, Horta the boar, and even Pacco the zebra, were rousing themselves from the effectd of the heat of the day. They were preparing to go down to the streams to drink and to wallow in their soothing depths. Tarzan must reach his destination quickly before night with its tropical suddenness dropped a blanket of darkness upon him, and before the fiercer jungle ones began to prowl for their supper. Already there were cries and rustlings to be heard in the tall grasses, already the birds were beginning to smooth their drooping meathers and twitter their sunset song. A little breeze revived Tarzan's spirit and he decided on the best and quickest way to travel.

Seizing a length of the tough creepers, which grew from the branches of a neighboring tree, he twisted it into a rough sort of rope and tied the girl to him by means of it. He held her steady with one arm while he used the other to swing them both into the branches of a great tree on the edge of the forest. Then those who had met Lord Greystoke in society in London during his two year stay there would have been shocked and amazed to see him absolutely revert to his ape training. He swung with long wonderfully graceful movements from branch to branch and from tree to tree, never once touching the ground, never once faltering as cleverly, as strongly, as completely confident of his footing as the best of his ape foster brothers. In this way Jane was bourne through a fairyland of green branches, and of distances shot with blue, red and gold of the dying sun, until finally they came to the rush bordered edges of the river, where it formed a little pool or inlet.

Meanwhile Rokoff had deliberately led the bull ape further and further away in a direction which he believed was near civilization, as represented by the line of march he remembered Gernot and Arabs were to take. Rokoff took his bearings by the sun, by the trees, by every bit of forest lore that he could remember, because he was a desperate man who realized that he must get out of the jungle at all cost. Just as he was about to despair, for he also realized that the day was drawing to its close and Queen La would perhaps grow suspicious and send out her warriors after him—the bull ape began to make strange cries and to attract his attention by pulling at his coat. The beast had been showing worry for some moments past, snuffling the air with his large ugly nostrils as if it detected the presence of an enemy. Now it showed such uneasiness that Rokoff almost lost his temper and raised his hand to strike him. A moment's reflection showed him how foolish this would be as the ape was so much stronger than he that he would probably tear him and bite him into shreds. So Rokoff used his brains instead and listened with all his might. The almost imperceptible sighing of the sunset breeze in the branches was the only thing that came to his ears.

He had not, like Tarzan, had the benefits of being brought up by a savage mother. He could not, with the reasoning powers of a man, combine the keen senses of the animal. Tarzan, could, like the jungle beasts detect the odor of footprints hours after they had passed. He could, of course distinguish between the different spoor, but through his sense of smell he was warned of the approach of strangers and enemies long before even his keen ears and eyes gave him the information.

However, somewhere in the past, the Russian remembered having read that the ear pressed to the ground will detect sounds quicker. He laid himself on a little knoll and stretched one ear to the grass. After a long time it seemed to him that he could distinguish the reoccurring sound of very distinct footsteps—more than one footstep. Hope sprang high in his breast. More than one man meant a caravan—a caravan would mean only one thing in that part of the world: Gernot and his ivory traders.

By signs and emphatic gestures Rokoff made the ape understand that these were friends to them both and, he added, to the queen—this he illustrated by pressing the bracelet she had given to his heart. The ape, who had been trained to understand gestures as well as language, and who knew the queen loved and trusted this man, and that he was her new favorite, finally allowed his scoldings and chatterings to subside and even climbed into a tree to get some food, while Rokoff sat on the knoll, his spear held tightly in his hand ready to welcome friend or foe.

Finally the footsteps grew clearly distinguishable and they kept measure to a plaintive sing-song in nasal tones—Arabs, there was no doubt of that. The listened had heard the marching ditty any number of times. He gave a hasty glance at the ape who was away up in the top branches of a tall tree eating a cluster of fruit. Then he ran as fast as he could to meet the column.

The first man he saw, sallow, fever ridden, and with torn and stained clothing, was Gernot, his long lost accomplice. Then Rokoff believed his luck had turned at last and that he was going to prove for once that he was a true soldier of fortune.

"Gernot, my friend!" he cried and fell into the Frenchman's arms.

"Nikolas, cher ami!" Gernot cried his amazement and seizing him kissed him upon both cheeks—a proceeding which the Russian returned with many embraces and pats on the back.

"You have saved my life!" he kept on repeating with tears of relief stealing down his cheeks.

No one noticed the bull ape who had hobbled up behind them and who stood without understanding all this strange noise, but when they had reached camp and Rokoff was being fed, he ungratefully kicked the poor ape for stealing a piece of bread and then laughed heartily as it ran off howling into the jungle.

The Frenchman, who was on his way to attack a village of the Waziri, burn it to the ground and steal its women and its ivory, was very glad to listen to the superior attractions of Opar.

"And I have something better than ivory for you, my friend," Rokoff told him. "What would you say to a treasure room lined with virgin gold and only a tribe of dwarfs to guard it? Also there is the matter of a savage queen who is not half as black as you would think—probably has a white father in her history—and will bring a pretty sum of money on the slave market."

Gernot thought pretty well of it, indeed—
[missing] by the magic th[missing] the two rascals
ha[missing] would even in the [missing]n.

Tarzan [missing] of thoughs was at [missing]
was making a bed of dried grasses and leaves for
Jane in the crotch of a tree. He had laid her on a
rock by the bank of the river where it made a deep
pool, half closed in by rushes, and he had bathed
her face and hands in the refreshing water—she
was almost wholly delirious and did not know
him, except at the briefest intervals.

Neither Tarzan, nor of course Jane had
noticed every now and then slight ripples in the
sluggish water of the pool which seemed to whip it
into life without the excuse of wind or of any
object which could be seen. Neither were these
movements like the sudden rings made by the
leaping of small fish.

Very much worried, Tarzan was busy with
his back turned, making as snug a nest for the
girl as he could. Jane was moaning and throwing
herself about restlessly, a prey to the workings of
her fevered brain. All at once in one of these
movements she rolled from the rock down to the
water's edge where she lay helpless half in the
pool.

Instantly it became alive with whithing
bodies, reptile-like tails and snapping jaws. It
was the home of Agri, the crocodile and his family.
Tarzan, hearing the sound of Jane's fall, turned
just in time to see Agri himself, with jaws dripping
yellow scuf and little pig eyes gleaming like coals,
hovering right over Jane's head with its glistening
curls.

CHAPTER V

FLAMES OF HATE

When Tarzan returned and saw the dripping jaws of Agri the crocodile open to swallow Jane as she lay unconscious and half in the water of the pool, he gave a terrible cry, half beast and half human, which sent the hideous shapes to churning the waters of the pool. Then, seizing a branch of the tree where he stood, he made a lightning swing over the spot where she lay and snatched her up as if she had been a feather.

He carried her to the couch of grass and leaves which he had made in the hollow of the tree, and tucked her in securely by fastening her with ropes made of the tough grass and the creepers. Feeling more secure on her account, he returned to the water's edge and began to dig and cut the bulbous roots he needed to make her well. But even then his task was not an entirely peaceful one, for once Agri stole up behind him, hoping to catch him unaware. He little realized that Tarzan, like all wild things, sensed the danger he could not see and so turned and faced the king of the crocodiles with angry eyes, and Agri, who like most of his kind was an arrant coward, thought it better to appear bent on something else as he slipped hastily into the pool.

Then in the branches above a pair of greenish eyes glowed and a spotted form which had followed him for miles in the treetops nervously gathered itself for a spring. It was

Sheeta the leopard. She was afraid of Tarzan, as all of the beasts of the jungle were, and for this reason perhaps bungled her spring just as he was rising to his feet. She missed and only grazed his arm with her sharp claws, but he seized her slender body in an iron grip and flung it far out into the pool to the waiting crocodiles.

Dusk was indeed almost upon him and he was anxious to reach Jane and give her the healing herbs, but when he climbed into the crotch of the tree, all he saw were the shreds of the rope with which he had bound her safely. The leaves and grass were scattered all over the ground below, and the girl had disappeared into the gathering darkness of the forest.

Over all hung the scent of the bull ape of Opar.

* * * * * * * *

In the camp of Gernot and the Arabs, Rokoff, inflamed by the cognac, was urging Gernot to postpone his expedition against the Waziri and to start immediately to go back Opar.

The flame of greed which smouldered in Gernot's sallow face found vent in words. He suddenly gave an order to his Arab lieutenant to gather the rest of the troop and that they would start immediately.

But the man hesitated. "It is perhaps not well that we venture too far in the forest with the dying of the sun, master," he observed.

"Coward!" Gernot silenced him. "You will not have a chance to show your bravery for we shall surprise them while they sleep!"

They had gone a few miles and were nearing a little clearing when they heard women's screams

43

mixed with uncouth cries and gibberings. The Arabs believing in evil spirits clasped their rifles closer and advanced more slowly. But Gernot and Rokoff, who were not afflicted with superstition, ran on ahead with Gernot's lieutenant, and in the clearing they came upon the bull ape carrying off the struggling Jane.

With a laugh of relief Rokoff raised his rifle and shot the ape. As he fell it released Jane who fled blindly right into their hands. She struggling with all her might but the three of them were more than a match for a sick girl and they half led her, half pushed her, to where the rest of the troop were waiting. Among these was the physician of the expedition. Even the two brutes who dragged her on realized that Jane was ill so they turned her over to his care. When they arrived in camp he laid her on a couch and gave her a potion to reduce the fever. Then as she moaned and clutched at her shoulder, he laid it bare and saw printed there in angry, inflamed lines the map of Opar which Rokoff had so cruelly cut in with the sharpened point of his buckle.

The Arab's withered face looked up at the two white men with an expression which made them avert their eyes. "I shall bathe this with a lotion which will efface it," was all he said, however, and left the tent to get some herbs and salves from his private store.

Immediately Rokoff went over to the table and procured a pencil and paper. While Gernot held the girl motionless, he carefully copied the map and then they both awaited with indifference the return of the physician—only at intervals they both stole glances at her—Rokoff openly, but Gernot just as often when his companion was not looking.

During this time Tarzan was following the scent and trail of the ape. When he neared the clearing he heard the mocking and scolding cries of a number of parakeets and other birds as they seemed to surround something which lay on the ground. As he drew near they scattered with harsh cries, flying so low in their curiosity that they nearly brushed his face, and then he saw the bull ape who lay grievously wounded with a gunshot in his shoulder.

The first instinct of the ape was to bare its teeth and make hostile demonstrations, but Tarzan uttered low, soothing sounds in the ape language and it paused and listened to him in astonishment. It finally let the strange Tarmangani carry him to the water's edge, bathe his wounds, bind them with leaves and revive him.

This Tarzan did that he might find out the whereabouts of Jane.

"Where is the she-Tarmangani who is my mate?" he demanded sternly of the ape.

With doleful moanings and mutterings, the big monkey clung gratefully to his rescuer and told him in ape language that Jane had been carried off by Rokoff and the Arabs and that, when he had attempted to fight Rokoff, the latter had shot him.

"I am Og, thy brother," whimpered the ape. "O, great Tarmangano, give me the chance to serve thee, to undo what I have done."

Tarzan patted him on the head and bade him lead them to the Arab encampment. "They'll make a fire to cook their evening meal; if you discover it, let me know," he said as he helped the ape into the branches of a big tree overhead and swung up himself afterwards.

45

It would have been indeed folly to trail anyone on the ground at that hour for the lions and other beasts were already a prowl searching for their supper. Only a short distance under him, Tarzan heard the roar of a hungry lion as he sprang and the cry of a springbob as he went down under those merciless claws. To the left of him near the pool he could hear two big cats snarling and fighting as to which one should have precedence at the drinking place. And all about him in the darkness the forest was alive after the torrid day—and the struggle for existence went on between the stronger and the weaker. Tarzan with his heart growing every moment heavier with fear Jane and loneliness for her presence was impeded by the darkness in which, in spite of his training, his human eyes could not see as well as those of the beasts. He was delayed also by having to stay a prisoner in a tree while he waited for some animal to move on from it, lay gorging on its repast, but still ugly enough to attack any intruder it might see.

But if the heart of Tarzan was heavy and pining for the girl, her's was no less so as she sat on the couch in the tent watching the two men as they laughed and drank in the firelight.

The medicine had relieved her fever enough so that she began to realize that she must make a supreme effort and escape at the first possible moment. Her beauty was a greater menace to her safety than the fever ever could have been. Summoning all her powers of acting to her aid, she smiled at the astonished Rokoff.

He was only too pleased at this sign of softening on her part and he asked her if she would not join them in some wine. Jane pretended that she was too weak to leave the couch and he brought her a goblet, unheeding of the jealous watchful eyes of Gernot, but the Russian had no intention of forcing his attentions on the girl just then. The wine was good and he returned to his drinking.

Jane's danger sharpened her wits and she noticed how longingly the Arab guard, who was to stay at the door of her tent all night, had looked at the wine which he might not drink. Now she beckoned to him in the shadow of the background and silently invited him to taste her cup. At first he hesitated, and then, with a wary eye fixed upon his masters as they crouched over the campfire he greedily drained it.

The girl, who was also watching, quickly waved him back and Rokoff happening to turn just then, caught her apparently in the act of drinking the last drop from her goblet. She nodded that she wanted more and he staggered over to fill it for her and whispered at the same time something in her ear which made her eyes blaze under her lowered eyelashes.

The second cup went the way of the first, and a third after it, as Jane each time summoned the Arab stealthily and made him drink it all. They were all getting very drowsy with the heat of the wine and the warmth of the camp fire which sent its smoke and light up through an opening in the top of the tent and thus was very earily seen by the watchers in the forest.

When the ape detected it, in his eagerness he forgot Tarzan's warning and dropped to the ground that he might proceed faster.

Immediately a huge beast rose up from the shelter of some bushes at his left and, trumpeting shrilly his annoyance, he charged right on the ape. It was Tantor the elephant as usual sulky at the presence of strangers.

The ape fled as fast as his shambling gait and his wound would allow but Tantor, who was getting angrier every minute, gained steadily upon him. In despair poor Og made a wild spurt and swung himself into the lower branches of a tree, but immediately the elephant charged the tree trunk, butting against it with all the strength in his huge body and the full grown trunk gave way as if it were the stem of a flower. The ape was spilled to the ground once more and had to run for his life.

Fortunately another tree was near and he leaped into its friendly branches. This time Tantor, fairly squealing his wrath, made shorter work of the same performance and this trunk went down even quicker than the first. With a howl for help which he hoped Tarzan would hear, Og fell out of the branches almost under the elephant's feet and the latter with a trumpet of rage curved his trunk to snatch him up.

"Tantor!" It was the voice of Tarzan, as he dropped from the branches and laid his hand soothingly, but at the same time commandingly, on the upraised trunk. "You must not harm this ape. He, too, is my friend. You two must be pals and help me to find my mate."

Tantor lowered his trunk and his little red eyes lost their fury.

"Come," coaxed Tarzan. "Kneel, that my new friend may mount you for he is sore and weary and has been wounded."

Tantor, whose disposition was easily turned from one extreme to another, nodded his big head as a sign that he understood and graciously allowed himself to be mounted.

It was well that they hastened for, in the

camp, one cup of wine had succeeded the other and Gernot and Rokoff were thinking the same evil thoughts and wondering how they would get each other out of the way, when fortunately for the girl, their attention was distracted by a terrific uproar outside. The shrill trumpetings of an exasperated elephant mingled with the crashing of trees and the tramplings of saplings brought the two men to their feet and they rushed outside in answer to the cries of the Arabs.

This was the chance Jane had been looking for. She quickly motioned the Arab guard toward the remnant of the bottle the two men had left behind. He drank it down at one gulp and sank stupefied on the couch by her side. Then she ran swiftly to where he had laid his gun, seized it and fled for her life out into the moonlit jungle. The Arabs were all gathered in a little group facing with their guns the fearful noises which were ringing through the forest. Gernot and Rokoff had gone ahead to investigate and the guard had sunk into a stupor and could not follow her, therefore she had a fair start and she made the most of it.

Heedless of any new danger she ran from what she very rightly held as the greatest of all, and so it happened that she found herself right in the path of a leopard who was stalking his prey. The beast made one spring for her and missed but before he could gather himself for another she raised her rifle and shot him in mid air.

The sound of the gun brought three people to the spot. Rokoff and Gernot, who had discovered her absence, and half killed the guard, and Tarzan, who came swinging through the branches. He arrived just in time to find her struggling in their grasp.

"Tarzan!" she screamed, as she fought

wildly. His answer was the battle cry of the apes as he leaped to the ground. But filled with the memory of his superhuman strength the two rascals fled, leaving Jane behind.

On the bank of the river where their camp was laid they paused for counsel.

"This man is of the devils, my friend!" said Gernot. "It is not for us to use ordinary means to rid ourselves of him."

"The woman is also a hellcat!" affirmed the Russian. "I am well rid of her. Let us destroy them both."

As he spoke, a bit of tree moss dropped on his shoulder. He picked it off and the dryness of it gave him an idea, at which he laughed and shrugged his shoulders unpleasantly.

"It has not rained for many months," he suggested "and the jungle is very dry, shall we burn it and them, eh, Gernot?"

"We can strike camp, cross the river on the logs and leave them cut off to be eaten by the flames—or the crocodiles. Ah, Oui cher ami!" agreed the Frenchman.

They hurriedly set to work on their evil task. As rapidly as possible they collected men and baggage and sent them across the river. Then they started the underbrush to burning in a dozen places before at least they themselves crossed to safety.

The wind was in their favor, and in what appeared to be only a few seconds, the bushes and even the trunks of trees were one roaring blood red inferno.

Tarzan, high up in the branches, with Jane in his arms, was blinded by a puff of smoke, scorched by a tongue of flame which crackled upward fed on the resin of the trunk, and found himself, before he hardly realized it, cut off in the midst of a fiery furnace.

In vain they tried to climb down the tree which now was all ablaze, they did not know which way to turn, and suddenly the bough on which they stood parted and dropped them both down into the hell of flame.

CHAPTER VI

THE IVORY TOMB

Tarzan held a corner of his leopard skin over the girl's face and fought his way through the roaring flames until he reached a little clearing where he could stop a moment and take breath.

Rokoff's work of setting the forest ablaze was complete. Each bush and every tree, parched and devoid of moisture through the long drought, crackled into flame as the slightest spark touched it. The fire was gaining at every instant. From the blazing undergrowth lions and leopards leaped terrified, with their coats singing as they ran. There was clearly no time to lose. Tarzan wrapped one arm around Jane and made a swing for the nearest tree which the flames had not reached yet. Once safe in its branches he lifted himself by means of his trusty rope to the next, and, thus from tree to tree he reached the river's edge. There the swiftly gathering flames behind him urged him to even greater action. Staking everything on one long swing of his rope, he caught it on the fork of a tree on the opposite bank and with a mighty exercise of his muscles which no ordinary man could hope to emulate, he swung himself and Jane clear across.

No wonder that Rokoff, Gernot and their Arabs paused on their march away from the river to shake their fists in the direction in where they thought he was being burned alive and to utter cries of triumph. The situation would have been fatal to any man not brought up among the jungle apes.

As they sank exhausted on the ground after the prodigious efforts they had made to reach safety, both Jane and Tarzan distinctly heard the trumpeting of an elephant not far away in the river.

"Tantor!" called Tarzan.

The big brute, who had started to roll over on his side and wallow, regardless of the frightened ape on his back and of possible crocodiles, straightened himself with a jerk and plunged across the remainder of the river in joyful answer to that friendly call. As he climbed up in the grassy bank of the river Tarzan and Jane met him and petted and caressed him. They were indeed glad to see their friend and to climb upon his broad back. The girl sat on top of his head while Tarzan directly behind her held her firm. The ape brought up the rear of the trio on the accommodating Tantor as they disappeared beneath the swaying trees of the forest.

Meantime Rokoff, Gernot and the Arabs had stopped to reconnoiter on a slight rise of ground and from that vantage point they saw a band of blacks going through the forest single file, bearing fine tusks of ivory. The men belonged to a tribe called the Waziri and immediately the cupidity of the Arab doctor was excited.

"Master," said he to Gernot, "let us attack their village for its ivory. They tell me there are great stores of it there and you yourself thought well of the plan when I first told it to you, before this other man (pointing to Rokoff) came."

"Oh, yes," answered Rokoff, "but it would take a mountain of ivory to equal the gold of Opar. Let us go on to Opar!"

But the Arabs felt differently about the matter. "The ivory is here, the gold is not! We want the ivory!" they cried in unison, and drawing to one side, with much muttering and brandishing of knives, they started to mutiny.

"This will never do," muttered Gernot to Rokoff. "We are miles from any white settlement and they will overpower us and seize all our provisions and weapons. I could curse their stupid yellow hides, but we must let them have their way."

He summoned the Arab doctor with a wave of his hand.

"You are right, mon vieux," he announced with apparent good nature. "We shall capture this village and the treasure of Opar can wait."

The ugly look left the doctor's face and he nodded his head in satisfaction.

With stealthy tread, the band of Arabs led by the two white rascals wound their way through the forest in the wake of the unsuspicious Waziri. But if the bearers of ivory did not heed them, another pair of eyes was watching. Tarzan, high up in a tree had spied his enemies and was trying to make out the nature of their suspicious movements.

Jane had complained of hunger and Tarzan had alighted with her from the elephant's back and sent Og, the bull ape ahead to find food. The two lovers, left alone amid the peaceful green forest, sat on a glossy bank to wait for the ape's return. The fire and smoke were all left miles back of them. Nature in that spot was beautiful and serene. Gay colored flowers bloomed in the luxuriant growth, bees and butterflies fluttered in the sunshine, while overhead, in the woodland, gorgeous birds flashed their wings in and out of the thick foliage and twittered their songs.

A great peace and happiness came over the girl. She leaned over and touched with her little hand the forehead of Tarzan as he sat at her feet, and the giant swept her into his arms and kissed her long and ardently.

"My dearest," said he, "we shall never be parted again?"

"Never," breathed Jane, as she clung stikk closer to him.

Og interrupted them by appearing with some cocoanuts, which he had obtained without much effort, as he was rather lazy. He had wandered through the forest until he had met another one of his own kind, swinging luxuriously in an ape swing composed of dried grasses and the tough creeping vines which hung from a tree.

This ape he waked from his comfort by appealing to him in the monkey language:

"Brother, I am hungry."

The big fellow blinked his eyes, reached up lazily and threw down such a shower of nuts from his storehouse that Og barely had time to dodge to avoid being hit. In fact the strange ape was rather mischievous after the manner of his kind, in his bombardment and took joy in the jumping around and the dodging of his needy brother. As quickly as possible, therefore, Og thanked him and ran off with an armful he had managed to salvage.

On these provisions, the three of them— Tarzan, Og and the girl—managed to make a very good meal and they felt much refreshed afterward and decided to keep on their journey. It was in order to reconnoiter that Tarzan once more ascended the tree, and as he let his eyes travel over the horizon he saw the treacherous band creeping through the underbrush.

Knowing the character of the men, Tarzan did not doubt for one moment that they were planning some deviltry.

"Let the ape guard you," he said to Jane. "I want to learn if that is Rokoff and his bandit friend raiding for ivory."

The girl was still a little afraid of being left alone with the bull ape, but Tarzan reassured her.

"Do not be afraid, my dearest," he said. "This ape knows you belong to me and would guard you with his life." He placed her hand on the big ugly forehead and it chattered its approval and looked at her with eyes of dog-like fidelity.

Jane was satisfied and Tarzan swung his way off among the trees to where he could get a better view.

It happened, however, that another pair of eyes was watching the prowling band of intruders. The brown sentinel of the Waziri who was hidden in the underbrush gazed upon them until he was sure of their purpose, and then he ran with such haste into the village that he dropped his long, heavy shield on the way.

He never stopped until he reached the doorway of the chief's house. There he kicked the sleeping sentinel into wakefulness and soon found himself in the presence of the head man of his tribe.

"Great One," he gasped with his breath coming in long stabs from his swift running. "Strangers armed with long firesticks are on the way here with ill will in their hearts and in great numbers."

The chief needed no second warning. He sounded the great drum in front of his tent, and at the sound all the village gathered.

"The first thing to do, O my children," said he, "is for the elders of the tribe and the women and children to hurry back as far as possible out of danger, and then we must safeguard our ivory treasure."

Accordingly the little band of noncombatants was sent out into the forest at the rear, while the men and boys under the direction of the chief began to bring out great armfuls of ivory and to deposit it in a huge long pit at the rear of the chief's hut in a special room built to accommodate this pit or rocky vault. And hardly had the last ivory tusk been lowered into its depths when the first shots of the attacking party were heard whistling through the thatched roofs of the village huts.

"And now set the trap for the rash fool who touches our treasure," cried the chief as he closed the vault and went over to a wooden cage containing three full grown lions which stood nearby. "Woe to him who dares try to reach the treasure!" he concluded as he connected the sliding door of the cage containing the fierce beasts with the door of the treasure chamber. "He who enters here will set free the lions at the same time."

Seizing his spear gave the signal to his men to advance against the enemy. But whirling spears are poor resistance against steel bullets, and in a very short time indeed the Arabs were in possession and the Waziri were put to flight with many of their number lying in the streets of their village dead or grievously wounded.

Rokoff and Gernot left the rest and entered the chief's hut, bent on finding the ivory ahead of the Arab doctor. They reached the door of the inner room when, to their amazenment, at the same time the door of the big cage shot up and three fierce lions bounded toward them. The two men slammed the door shut and latching it hastily, fled in terror to the street.

Tarzan from his tree watched them run for their lives. He heard Rokoff command Gernot to get enough Arabs to go back in the hut, and as the Frenchman left to round up his followers, he saw his opportunity to follow Rokoff and recover his papers. He dropped down from his tree and stole swiftly after him as he turned once more to enter the village.

If Tarzan had known the danger that was threatening Jane he no doubt would have turned back, but he was too far away to hear her cries. The fleeing Waziri had overtaken her, and the ape, warned by their scent, had lifted her up into a tree. There both girl and monkey cowered in the cleft of the big limbs, while below the tribe danced a war dance and hurled their spears at them.

"Come down, Queen of the Arabs!" they screamed at Jane in their dialect which naturally she could not understand, but their threatening gestures were only too plain as well as the rain of javelins with which they punctuated them.

Jane's skin, so much fairer than their own, made them think her the ruler of the lighter skinned Arabs who were plundering their village. They wished to take revenge on her, and half understanding their purpose, she shivered and clung to the tree, trying to hide behind its leaves.

Finally, a spear driven more accurately than the rest hit the bull ape in the chest and his screams of rage echoed through the forest as he lost his balance and fell from his bough. Jane, wide eyed with terror on her limb of the tree, saw a black shape climbing toward her with outstretched hand. With a shriek she closed her eyes and blindly jumped, scarcely knowing what she did. As she fell through space she thought of Tarzan, who at that moment was entering the door of the chief's hut in pursuit of his bitter enemy, Rokoff.

So intense were his emotions in fact, on beholding once more the man who had robbed him of his valuable papers and tried to kill him and Jane, that he never noticed behind him the sneaking figure of Gernot, who, revolver in hand, had come on ahead of his Arabs. Tarzan slammed the door of the hut shut and with a savage cry of joy hurled himself straight at Rokoff's throat. The Russian went down under him and the two fought savagely all over the floor choking and even biting each other, until at last Tarzan triumphantly ripped off Rokoff's money belt and secured the precious papers.

He barely had time to throw Rokoff off to one side and secure the papers before the door was again violently thrown open and Gernot was upon him. But only for a moment. Tarzan overcame the slighter man with even greater ease, and as Rokoff picked up a rudely carved seat to throw it at him he countered in a much quicker manner by hurling the now limp Gernot through the air at the Russian and knocking him clean into the street through the open doorway again. Then Tarzan flung himself on the half beaten Frenchman as the latter started to draw his gun and laid him flat once more; he recovered a second paper, that which Gernot had drawn from the sketch on Jane's back of the treasure house of Opar.

Seeing Gernot limp and apparently unconscious, Tarzan started to find his way by opening the door leading to the ivory vault. Fortunately, he did this very slowly for the first few inches showed him the lions leaping against the door in their eagerness and snarling and fighting among themselves for the first chance to reach the intruders.

Tarzan hastily slammed the door shut, but did not have a chance to bolt it, because of the frantic lunges the lions made against it which required all his strength to hold it with both hands. He was straining so hard against the flimsy structure that he never noticed the stealthy movements of Gernot until suddenly the latter recovered his revolver, fired, and simultaneously with the stinging pain from the wound in his shoulder, Tarzan relaxed his hold against the door and the lions burst in upon them.

CHAPTER VII

THE JUNGLE TRAP

Tarzan, with his hand clapped to the flesh wound in his shoulder, felt the door give way and saw the lions dash into the hut. But swift as they were, he was quicker. He threw the door wide open and flattened himself between it and the wall so that the hungry animals dashed past him in hot pursuit of Rokoff, who had come back and who stood in the farther entrance. With a yell of terror the Russian fled into the open, and, with the lions almost at his heels, he tore across the compound and hoisted himself into a tree just in time to escape their teeth and claws.

Tarzan was left alone in the chief's hut with the prostrate Gernot, and was about to turn on him and give him further punishment for so treacherously attacking him from behind, when yells and savage cries warned him of the approach of a band of Waziri warriors.

The more daring of the brown men had managed to shake off their pursuers and to turn back toward the village. They saw Rokoff in the tree, held captive by the lions below him, and they rushed out of the chief's hut to see whether the ivory was safe.

At the sight of Tarzan and of the open door behind him, their fear changed to anger and they started to attack him.

"Thief! Jackal!" they cried in dialect, which he understood perfectly, and they raised their spears threateningly.

But Tarzan held up his hand.

"Hark to me brothers," he began in their own language. "I am no thief, but behold the one who is. This white stranger is one of the two who planned the destruction of your homes and to drive your wives and children into slavery. Behold I have beaten him so that he lies on the ground, and as for the other robber who was also a leader of the Arabs, for him I loosed the lions and they drove him from here and saved your treasure. Hail brothers and know me for Tarzan of the Apes and your friend."

The Waziri had listened to his speech in wonder. Now their glances, roving around, verified his words, for the trap door which concealed the treasure had not been moved. At the mention of his name the light of recognition came into the leader's face. He stood before his men with arms extended.

"Take heed, all of you," he cried, "He is big 'Bwana,' friend of the jungle." And the tribe who knew him by reputation acclaimed him as their protector and friend.

Meanwhile the noise of shots which Rokoff was firing at the lions from his perch in the tree brought the Arabs in the distance to his help in double quick time. Tarzan and the Waziri heard their shouts and the tribesmen were all for rushing out and attacking immediately, but Tarzan's common sense prevailed.

"No," he told them, "you are not strong enough. You cannot overpower them for they have guns. We must steal out of the village at the rear into the jungle and I will show you a way to defeat your enemies."

So the little band of brown warriors retreated with Tarzan into the jungle just as the

Arabs rescued Rokoff from his tree after killing one of the lions and driving the others off.

As soon as the Russian was once more on firm earth, he cried: "Gernot is still in that hut and maybe the lions are after him. We must go back and try to save him!"

They proceded with levelled guns back to the village and the chief's hut. Cautiously they pushed open the door, but all the lions had left at one time. Gernot lay, more stunned than hurt, save for his bruises. In fact, gathering courage from the fact that Tarzan had been forced to leave him behind, he was even then struggling to his feet.

The two partners in crime embraced like two long lost brothers. But their joy was of short duration.

"Have you the paper safe?" asked Rokoff, speaking of the map of Opar.

"No, that accursed devil took it from me!" was Gernot's answer, and in his turn he asked, "Have you the formula?"

"By the holy images, no!" cried Rokoff. "That caveman robbed me of it!"

"Robbed you of the formula? Why, that is our fortune! Why did you let him have it?"

"For the same reason, you idiot, that you let him get the map of Opar from you."

Matters threatened to become strained between the pair.

Rokoff shrugged his shoulders.

"Oh, well, there's no use crying over spilled milk and pulling each other's hair out," he growled. "The thing to do is to plan how to recover them."

"Ah, oui, mon ami, but how?" answered the Frenchman.

They were in the midst of a heated discussion when the Arabs, who also had been taking counsel, approached and spoke through their mouthpiece, the doctor:

"We want the ivory! Will you give it to us or do we have to fight for it?"

"There is no question of the right thing to do," Rokoff interrupted him. "We must get the papers back from Tarzan and start for Opar immediately."

But the Arabs could not see it that way. They pushed past into the inner room and started to raise the trap door from the vault to remove the ivory. Gernot thereupon became almost frantic.

"That is it, dig your own graves, oh, you pigs, you savages!" he shrieked at them. "Here is your enemy with a paper that will bring the whole French army against us and you will never see your wives or your little ones again—nor shall I see Paris and the millions which I am willing to share with you. And yet, like fools, you quarrel over a few pieces of ivory, like dogs over carrion. As for me, I am through with you! I leave you to your fate!"

His almost hysterical pleading had its effect. The Arabs stopped and listened to his words. Maybe he was right. If so, they would be caught and hanged like dogs for helping him carry out some orders which were not agreeable to the great French chief. But if they could overtake the ape man they could steal back the papers to make them safe. It paid to be on the sure side—and after all there was the gold of Opar to console them for the loss of the ivory. And if they did not heed the white chief they would not live to enjoy either, so perhaps it was best to give up the elephants' tusks, for the time being at least, and to follow the trail of the stranger.

They sat in council and listened to Gernot and Rokoff.

Meanwhile in the forest the rest of the Waziri band was attacking the tree where Jane cowered among the branches, more dead than alive with fear at their strange gestures and cries. And then, to her greater terror, she saw a fierce looking brown man climbing up her tree with a dirty hand extended in her direction. Panic stricken and not realizing what she was doing she leaped into space and fell downward through the branches, landing with a splash and an impact which almost drove the breath from her into a sort of little pond which ran alongside the bank on which the tree stood.

Fortunately the body of water, although not wide, was fairly deep. Jane escaped with a dunking when she might easily have dashed her brains out is a shallower stream. She was a splendid swimmer and made her way to the bank where she emerged dripping only to fall into the hands of the exulting Waziris who formed a ring and did a war dance around her and the ape whom they already held captive. At the same time, they began to intone the death chant of their tribe and the monkey and the girl, crouched in the center of the ring, watched with terror stricken eyes their preparations.

"The Arabs have conquered us and stolen our spoils—but we have their queen—. She shall taste the brew that she made us drink and feel in her body the pains that she has made our brave ones suffer ere she goes to the hands of her ancestors."

This was the burden of their song and the barbaric cadences of it fell on Tarzan's ears as he dropped down from a tree into a clearing where they were holding their cruel dance. The Waziri raised their spears against him but he held them back with a wave of his hand.

"Stop brothers!" he cried in their own tongue as he had spoken to the rest of the tribe and, in sheer surprise at hearing their own dialect, they paused and listened to him.

"Why have you taken this girl prisoner?"

"She is the Arab queen!" spoke up the leader. "She has brought death and destruction on our tribe."

Tarzan laughed. "I am Bwana, friend of the jungle," he retorted. "The maiden is no queen of the Arabs, but my queen. Your chief knows me for a friend and he understands," and to clinch his words he made the signal of friendliness,

By this time the remainder of the Waziri had caught up with Tarzan and they confirmed his statements. The Waziri therefore let Jane and the ape go free and the girl rushed into Tarzan's arms.

"You have saved me again, my hero!" she murmured against his shoulder. "If we ever leave this dreadful jungle I will show you how I can repay your love and devotion."

Tarzan kissed her long and tenderly.

"There is work to be done my dearest," he answered, as he held her from him and looked into her blue eyes, "and you must wait my return and be brave. I know that nothing can happen to me now that I have you once more. I feel as if I bore a charmed life, and I know that I shall come back to you safe, but these poor children need my help and you must be brave and stay here with your little court, of my queen—and your ladies." He pointed to the women of the tribe who quickly came forward and surrounded the strangely beautiful white "queen."

Then to the men of the tribe Tarzan spoke.

"Oh, men of the Waziri, hark to me and obey! Get strong saplings and lion strings and I will show you how to conquor your enemies with sticks that spit fire."

The Waziri did as they were told. Each man unwound from his belt the strong cord made of sinews which they used in their traps, and the boys of the tribe scattered far and near and collected dozens of young saplings.

Then Tarzan whittled and shaped these so he could fasten a tightly drawn string to either end, and in this manner he instructed the Waziri in the art of using a bow, and he fashioned also some sharp pointed arrows which he gave to the tribesmen as fast as he could make them so when nighttime drew near they had quite a goodly store.

"I leave my queen to your care," Tarzan admonished the female Waziri, as he left Jane in their midst and set forth with all the men of the tribe, except the very young boys, fully armed each with his bow and arrows and fully determined to win back their ivory and household gods.

And so Rokoff and the Arabs, who together with Gernot were proceeding through the forest, all of a sudden were attacked by a cloud of murderously stinging arrows from the trees overhead.

Tarzan had told the Waziri:

"Never shoot your arrows while they're looking up at you and keep back among the foliage."

Therefore the Arabs could not imagine for a moment who it was who so mysteriously attacked them. They began to search, and Tarzan, seeing their fear and confusion gave the signal and another arrow sped forth with such good aim that it pierced one of the Arabs through the heart. The rest of them were thrown into a superstitious panic and, after several of their number had been severly wounded and they had not been able to get view of a single enemy, they fled toward the village in spite of anything that Gernot or Rokoff could do to stop them.

They had not gone far, however, when a single arrow whistling through the woods, this time not from above, killed one of the Arabs by passing right through his heart. The arrow had been fired near at hand. The Arabs were encouraged by the fact that it did not come from on high. They beat the bushes and produced the astonished Professor Porter, Jane's father. The aged scientist had been trying to find some trace of his daughter whom he had heard was with Tarzan. On the way, even in his anxiety, he could not forego the pleasure of capturing and analyzing the strange beetles and insects with which the forest was plentifully supplied. And it was while reaching down for a bright hued caterpillar that the professor spied a bow and arrow lying on the ground.

He had not seen one for years, not since, in fact, he had belonged to a Kentish archery club. With that bland and childlike smile which made him resemble nothing so much as a big overgrown boy, he picked up the bow and fitted the arrow to it with that precision which characterized him in all things and let fly with no particular aim at all. He was brought to a sudden realization that he was not alone in the forest by the rough grasp of two dirty Arabs on his person. Protesting wildly and volubly, he was dragged through the brush until he found himself in the presence of Rokoff.

"Well, this is a bit of luck!" chirped the professor, as he beamingly rushed forward and seized his prospective son-in-law's hands in both of his.

But Rokoff eyed him coldly. "Things have changed between us," he remarked curtly. "You just now shot one of my Arabs with your arrows. I am glad I caught you. Take him away men! We shall lodge him underground in the village."

Protesting and struggling, the dumb-founded professor was dragged away and the band pursued its retreat toward the village.

While both the Waziri and the Arabs marched toward the village, Jane had gone a little way into the forest with one of the young boys left in charge of the women. Mombo, the youth, wanted to show her an ape who was a particular friend of his and Jane, who had learned from Tarzan to lose a great deal of her fear of the ugly but intelligent beasts, watched Mombo play with the ape as it swung back and forth in its rude swing among the creepers, and even patted the strange animal herself.

She grew tired after a while, and walked a little to one side where the medicine man of the tribe crouched over a drum which he beat continuously with a monotonous tom-toming to attract the favor of the gods for the departed warriors. There was something uncanny about his fixed and glassy eyes and yet something which drew her with a power which gained the victory over her repulsion. If the girl had only known it, this was the hypnotic power of the man who kept beating the drum, looking straight into her eyes with his glassy and beckoning orbs until little by little she crept towards him, through treacherous undergrowth, unheeding the brambles, the briars or the poisonous growth, until suddenly she found herself caught in the coils of something worse even than one of the great snakes, for it was what is known as the death vine which clings to its victims and keeps enlacing them with its coils, like those of the octopus, until all life and feeling is crushed out with the breath of the victim.

But as Jane felt its clinging tendrils spread themselves around her slender young body it was already too late for her to do anything to save herself. Higher and higher crept the rank growth shutting her in like the coils of a serpent, crushing the breath for which she fought with anguish, and with the blood pounding in her ears she still heard the monotonous tom-toming and saw the relentless eyes of the medicine man as through a mist.

Back in the village, the Arabs had decided to camp for the night and give the bad spirits a chance to disappear with the dawn, but, whatever plans they had were dissipated by Rokoff, who dashed out to reconnoiter and as hastily ran back with the news that Tarzan and almost the whole tribe of the Waziri were close at hand and prepared to attack. As he sprang forward to report to Gernot he had to run over the trap door of bamboo which covered the ivory treasure. The door had been half replaced by the Arabs and so Rokoff fell through it down into the deep ivory pit.

He had barely been drawn out of it and the cover pushed partly over the opening when two lions raced into the village driven by fear of the approaching forces. They dashed over the half closed trap door, even as Rokoff had done, and before the Arabs even had a chance to fly for their lives the trap gave way and both animals fell way down into the pit with the ivory.

That gave Gernot his great idea. The trap was readjusted in such a manner that it appeared safe but was not—over its surface he ordered leaves and grasses strewn, then very quickly, for there was no time to lose, he ordered Rokoff to tie a flag of truce to a stick and when Tarzan shouted, "If you do not surrender, we will shoot you with flaming arrows!" the Russian waved this white flag of truce as a sign that they surrendered.

Tarzan therefore came forward and, leaving his squad of men with drawn bows and arrows at the edge of the compound, he ran lightly across it over the hidden trap door—and as this gave way with a sickening crack, he was sent hurtling downward into the pit where the lions were snarling and leaping up against the rocky sides.

Above: Elmo Lincoln as Tarzan with Edgar Rice Burroughs, the creator of Tarzan. *Below:* A lobby card.

Louise Lorraine as Jane and Elmo Lincoln as Tarzan

Above: The cast and crew. *Below:* Tarzan and Jane.

CHAPTER VIII

THE TORNADO

As Tarzan fell into the pit containing the two lions, there was a flash from Gernot's revolver and one of them fell dead. Rokoff turned to his companion in amazement, but the Frenchman cried:

"Don't kill him! We didn't stop to think, if the lions eat him we shall have no chance to recover the formula!"

Struck by the justice of this remark, Rokoff bent anxiously over the edge and watched Tarzan struggling with the remaining lion.

"You fellows make a rope of your sashes—I'm going down after him!" he cried, but before he had a chance to put this plan into operation there was a cry of victory from below—the lion, who was a coward, had turned from Tarzan's vigorous onslaught and, bleeding with many knife wounds, it fled down the tunnel and Tarzan after it.

This did not suit the watchers at all—for they certainly did not want their enemy to escape, bearing the valuable papers.

Rokoff was the first to figure out a solution. "The women and children of the Waziri are gone," he said. "This tunnel must lead to a spot of safety. We must find that spot."

"Well," answered Gernot, "I for one don't want to jump down into that dark vault. I am not Tarzan and that lion may be lying somewhere concealed in the dark shadows."

What plans the pair might have adopted

were interrupted by a rain of arrows from the Waziri outside. They had grown tired of waiting for Tarzan, and losing faith in him, they determined to carry on the battle themselves.

There were more savage war cries and another shower of arrows. The Arab doctor, Gernot's lieutenant, threw up his arms and fell down with an arrow through his heart. Several other members of the expedition were grievously hurt and Gernot escaped by the fraction of an inch.

"En avant, my children!" he called to his Arabs and they charged from the village and attacked the the black men gave way and ran back into the woods with the Arabs on their trail.

It was in the same part of the forest that the tunnel ended and Tarzan swung himself up into the trees that he might be out of the reach of his enemies. As he made his way from branch to branch he became conscious of moans like those of a woman in deadly agony, and, hastening his footsteps, he parted the branches and to his horror saw Jane in the strangling clutch of the death vine, while her hypnotized eyes never left those of the wicked medicine man who crouched over his magic cauldron.

The smile on the repulsive tattooed face of the medicine man caused Tarzan's blood to boil with indignation and with one leap, he gained the earth and at the same time gave the medicine man a mighty blow which sent him headlong into a little stream which was behind him. With every expression of tenderness Tarzan released Jane from the vine which was strangling her to death and, as she lay limp and fainting in his arms, he covered her dear face with kisses. But she did not respond, her eyes were closed and she remained lifeless. Seriously alarmed, Tarzan now laid her on the grass and wet her forehead with cooling water from the stream. Even then she did not stir—not even when he rolled her eyelids from her eyes and tried to waken some expression in her death-like face.

A chuckle from the bushes behind him made him turn hastily just in time to see the horrible face of the medicine man rejoicing in his suffering. Then and then only, did he realize that his beloved was still under the influence of the evil man's hypnotic influence and that he alone could awaken her.   Just as he came to this conclusion, and made a threatening gesture in his direction the black man made a hasty dive through the bushes and disappeared in the stream, swimming away for all he was worth. Like a flash Tarzan went after him and then followed one of the most difficult races around the rocks, in and out of rushes, with the medicine man diving and disappearing only to reappear in a totally opposite direction, until finally Tarzan caught him and held him under water until limp and exhausted he did his bidding.

Dragging him back none too gently to where the girl still lay unconscious on the grass, he ordered the spell to be removed under threat of instant death. The medicine man suddenly dipped his hand in the brew which was steeming in the pot and sprinkled her with a few drops of it. The first time she moaned and remembering the vine, she twisted and cried out as if it were still around her. Then he reached into the caldron and sprinkled her again, and then she remembered nothing, but awoke as if she had been dreaming and threw herself into Tarzan's arms.

The medicine man profited by this diversion

to make an exceedingly rapid escape and fled back through the forest, never stopping until he heard a fusilade of shots and savage cries, and then a silence broken by a man's voice.

It was Gernot and the few remaining Arabs in his command reproving Rokoff as he kicked and turned over on their backs the Waziri dead and wounded. The medicine man decided to hide in the bushes and watch developments.

"Why waste time with these savages?" the Frenchman inquired peevishly, "when it is Tarzan that we want?"

Rokoff straightened himself up from a prolonged examination of a Waziri warrior whose face was disfigured with blood from a big gaping wound.

"Die you swine!" he gave the poor black a last kick—then to the impatient Gernot he answered:

"How little you understand our enemy my friend! Tarzan is clever enough to stain his body in order to escape us and I am taking no chances."

At this point a twig crackled under the medicine man's feet and he had no choice but to come out into the open. He crouched down on his haunches and crept, much as a dog might, toward the two white men.

At the sight of him two of the wounded Waziri warriors rose half way on their elbows and howled their laments in unison.

"Ai woe! Oh woe!" they cried. "We have been set upon and destroyed. The big Bwana betrayed us and is responsible for our wounds and our dead!"

They crept toward the medicine man and embraced his feet. His face grew convulsed with rage at the suffering of his tribesmen. He turned to the two white men, drawing himself up half proudly and half with a gesture of appeal.

But Gernot and Rokoff were paying no attention to him.

"They blame Tarzan for the whole trick," the latter cried, triumphantly. "We'll switch the tribe to our side, then Tarzan cannot escape us."

"Good!" approved Gernot, and he came forward with his oily hypocritical smile and took the medicine man's withered hands in his.

"Oh, father," he said. "I see you know your real enemy! He has bewitched us and laid a wicked spell on our Arabs as well as on your tribe, let us then join hands and swear to be avenged on him."

"My gods will help you," the medicine man answered solemnly as he raised one of the Waziri wounded. Rokoff, quick to seize the opportunity, ordered the Arabs to take care of the remaining few and those who were able to march formed in single file and were supported, as best they could be by the others, for it was growing late in the day and they wished to make as much progress as possible before nightfall.

But as they left the spot where the encounter had taken place, the bushes parted cautiously and the bull ape's face peered through to note their numbers and the direction they took, and then he ran as fast as he could to find Tarzan and to warn him of the plot between the Arabs and the Waziri.

The little group of remaining Arabs and blacks had not gone far, however, before the wounds and the smell of blood attracted a band of hungry lions. The trembling natives heard the roar, first of one beast and then of another, answering it nearer. Then there was a rush through the underbrush and two lions, followed by their mates, charged the line of march and, seizing their victims, bounded away through the jungle. Rokoff was knocked flat but otherwise unhurt; Gernot, who was ahead, managed to fire his revolver at the fleeing animals and then both he and Rokoff took to their heels. Abandoning the rest they made their escape just as fast as their legs could carry them.

Meanwhile Tarzan and Jane, forgetting all save their great love, stood clasped in each other's arms silent for a long time, and just content to be once more together.

Finally he roused himself and taking the parchment from his belt he showed her the formula.

"With this, my dearest, you and I can both be rich and happy," he declared. "No wonder these dogs wanted to steal it from me. It's value is priceless."

Jane pressed her cheek lovingly against his. "Tarzan, dear," she ventured coaxingly. "Now that you have this evidence can't we get out of this awful jungle?"

Tarzan did not answer. His gaze was fixed in the deep blue of the sky, the green and gorgeous colored distance of jungle. He contrasted its brilliant butterflies and flowering vines, its bright hued birds, its sunlit sky with the crowded London streets and the gray fog-like vistas which to him spelled the cramping influence of civilization. Then once more he looked down at Jane. To live in continual adventure, in continual danger of one's life might be wonderful to a giant as strong and fearless as he was, but she was a delicately reared woman.

"I'm longing for a dress and—and a chance to comb my hair," Jane was coaxing him. She ran her fingers over its curly luxuriance. "I tried to comb it with some long thorns I found, but Tarzan dear, it hurt awfully and didn't seem to do much good except to pull out the hair."

He drew her to him and kissed the tangled brown locks. "Yes, dear, we'll go back," he agreed. "It is the only thing to do now, for I want you for my very own, for my dear wife."

A crashing through the underbrush startled them. It was the lions, and, fleeing before them, they heard the bull ape giving a cry of distress at every leap he made.

Tarzan swung Jane up into the boughs of a tree and ran to the assistance of his faithful friend. He arrived just in time to save him from the charge of a big lion which had separated from the pack and the animal was put to flight by Tarzan with an ugly knife wound in its side, obtained when it charged him.

"You have saved me again from Numa, master," the ape whimpered gratefully, and he told him of the treachery of the Waziri who had already forgotten all his kindness to them and sided with his enemies to destroy him.

"That is the way among men, Og," answered Tarzan sadly. "Not among apes or the jungle animals, and that is why I prefer the jungle. It is only man who repays kindness with treachery, and they call superior beings—ah, well, I suppose we cannot change the world."

He swung himself into a tree with the ape and they started toward the one where Jane sat waiting for him in the crotch of a big limb. Neither of them noticed a cruel spotted shape which crept along the leafy boughs toward the girl, and Jane was smiling happily to herself and thinking of the man she loved and so was unconscious of the danger creeping stealthily toward her until, with a snarl, the leopard sprang through the branches and bore her to the ground.

Her scream was echoed by Tarzan's cry as he swung down by her side, and, seizing the slender cat-like form of the leopard, he flung it far into the underbrush and anxiously felt all over her for broken bones and scratches from the cruel claws. So engrossed was he, and so frightened was the girl, that neither of them noticed the approach of Rokoff and Gernot, who, seeing Tarzan alone and off his guard, promptly opened fire and the giant fell with a wound in his arm almost in the same spot where the other bullet had only recently been removed. The pain was so great that Tarzan lay on the ground semi-unconscious, and the Waziri who came straggling up in answer to Rokoff's call easily overpowered him and bound him securely.

Jane, who had started to run as fast as she could when she saw she could be of no help and that her presence might hinder Tarzan, did not get very far. Rokoff plunged into the scrub growth after her and dragged her forth brutally. Then, while Rokoff and the Arabs bound her also, he turned Tarzan on his back and searched thoroughly for his papers.

He uttered an exclamation of triumph and then one of rage. Turning to Gernot, he cried:

"I have the formula here, but he has destroyed the map of Opar!"

Gernot showed his wolf-like teeth in a snarl of rage. "We'll kill him for that!" he answered.

The medicine man now approached and thrust his lean and hideously marked face to within an inch of Tarzan's.

"Hee-hee! Hoo-hoo!" he taunted, then he approached the Frenchman and, making a bow with his palms to his forehead, he said something to him in a low tone.

Gernot's evil laugh rang out.

"Bring your prisoner along, Nikolas," he shouted. "We're going to give him what he deserves and what this tattooed gentleman suggests. We are going to burn him at the stake according to the Waziri custom."

Jane gave a sob of despair, but all her struggles and those of Tarzan were in vain and the coming of sundown found the blacks gathered in a dancing, shrieking circle around Tarzan, who, bound to a stake with faggots at his feet, waited for the torch of sacrifice to be applied.

The girl was tied to a tree nearby, and every now and then the medicine man would come to her and exult in her anguish as he watched her lover vainly trying to free himself in the midst of the circle of whirling black men.

"Tarzan, oh Tarzan!" cried Jane, for at least the hundredth time, as she strained against her own bonds. A little cool wind had sprung up and blew the tendrils of her hair into her tear-blinded eyes.

Suddenly he answered her, and there was a queer note of exultation in his voice, so that Jane thought for one moment he had gone mad.

"Look—look at the sky!" he cried in English.

She did so, and then she understood. Heavy, black clouds were piling up with alarmingly rapidity. Jagged flashes of lightning tore rents in the sky. A dreadful storm, perhaps a tornado, was well under way. At any other moment Jane would have been frightened to death. As it was now, Tarzan's greater danger drove all else from her mind. She raised her hands to Heaven and called to the medicine man:

"See, the gods may avenge my mate!"

The medicine man at first laughed and then, with one look at the threatening sky, he rejoined the others. They stopped their song and dance of death to apply their burning torches to the faggots placed around Tarzan's feet and the flames sprang up, caressing his limbs and reaching out their long scorching arms to his face and hair.

Jane shrieked her agony and raised once more her eyes to Heaven.

"Oh, God, send—oh, send the storm!" she moaned, and as if in answer to her prayer, the heavens opened and the trees bent to earth in the grip of a giant wind which nothing could resist and down, as if the very flood gates of Heaven had given way, came the solid wall of blinding rain which accompanies a tornado.

Trees were uprooted in the path of the wind, the rain swept all before it like a solid wall of water. The singing, dancing savages fled before it, dragging Jane with them and leaving Tarzan to his fate.

Suddenly there was a terrible blinding glare of lightning and with it a crash of thunder that shook the very earth, and the tree to which Tarzan was bound, struck to its core crashed down, and buried him under its branches.

CHAPTER IX

FANGS OF THE LION

The sky seemed to open with a tremendous glare of lightning, with which was mingled a mighty crash of thunder, and the bolt which sent the tree down on Tarzan also laid the medicine man low.

Fortunately Tarzan was merely imprisoned by the branches which were easy for him to remove, and, what was a great deal more fortunate, the fall freed him from his bonds. The rain was coming down in almost a solid sheet, and he could make out the form of the medicine man as he lay groaning and praying to his gods.

Any one else would have left the treacherous brown man to die of fright and exposure, but not the big hearted Tarzan. He exerted all his strength and freed him from the trunk of the tree which was pinning him down and bore him in his arms to a place of safety.

After that he made his way to the chief's hut where he felt sure they had taken Jane. He approached warily and applied his ear to the thatch. He heard Rokoff and Gernot quarrelling about what they were to do with Jane, and then he heard a cry from the second room of the hut where the Professor had been imprisoned ever since the battle. The aged scientist had recognized his daughter's voice and burst into the room.

There were two exclamations of joy:

"Jane!"

"Daddy!"

The professor folded his daughter in his arms for the first time since the wreck of the Lady Alice. It was indeed a joyful moment for them both, but it lasted all too short a time, for Rokoff brutally intervened and trust them apart. When he seized Jane by the arm, he hurt her so that she screamed with pain and, Tarzan forgot all caution and burst through the thatched wall of the hut with murder blazing in his eyes.

But Rokoff and Gernot were no heroes. They did not want to face Tarzan unless they had a stout band of warriors at their backs. With the most undignified speed they fled from the hut disappearing down the darkness of the village street in the blinding rain.

"We cannot spend much time in conversation," Tarzan said to the father and daughter. "I must run after those villains before they escape in the night."

Jane clung to him. "Oh, Tarzan, dear, please be careful!" she cried. "They are armed and will kill you!"

He thought a moment. "I am not worrying about myself, dear," he answered, "but about you. I am going to put in the ivory vault where you will be safer from the storm as it is underground. As for myself, I must get the sheepskin from Rokoff before he can reach their airplane, which I overheard them say they had left near here."

He would not be moved by Jane's pleadings not to be left alone, for he felt he owed it to his government not to fail in regard to the formula, so aided by the professor, he lowered Jane into the pit, and then the old man himself followed her down into its semi-darkness.

Tarzan disappeared in the mist and rain of the village street which was so dense that he did not see a group of Waziri, led by Rokoff, making for the pit from a neighboring hut whence they had observed all. Just as they reached the edge of the vault and were preparing to jump in, there was a shriek from Jane and a snarl from a lion who had taken refuge from the storm in the cavern.

Two of the Waziri who were nearest the edge fell into it in their terror and the lion turned and chased them. Jane and her father were thoroughly grateful for this diversion and ran on toward the tunnel's mouth praying there were no more lions or other wild beasts in their path.

Through openings in the rocky roof they could see that the tornado had passed on elsewhere. Gradually the rain stopped. As the wind died down the sky grew brighter with the approach of dawn until, as they reached the entrance of the tunnel, and saw the green of the jungle before them, the sky became flecked with vivid gold and rose, the birds wakened in a grand chatter and swung from their perches in the vines overhead. It was another fine and beautiful day.

Jane and the professor stood quietly admiring the wonder of it, when all of a sudden a black, hairy shape flung itself at their feet from the branches overhead, frightening the old man almost out of his senses and even causing the brave girl to start nervously.

It was Og, the faithful bull ape, who welcomed them with discortant cries expressive of his great joy.

The professor sat down rather weakly on a grassy mound and wiped the perspiration from his forehead.

"My dear—how that—er—monkey startled me!" he exclaimed, "and now that I think of it, it must be time for breakfast. Those damned savages only had some bananas and dried fish in their hut all those hours I was shut in there. The smell of the fish was enough for me—and as I have often told you, bananas are most indigestible."

Jane had to laugh at her father's peevish tone. If the old professor stayed years in the jungle he never could become a sport in the sense of ceasing to demand his comfort, come what might.

"Be patient, daddy," she soothed him. "This kind ape will help us rejoin Tarzan, and will find some food for us."

The professor grunted. "Well—I hope he doesn't bring us bananas," he observed ungraciously.

It was not bananas that the ape brought this time—perhaps he understood the Professor's aversion. He soon returned with several large cocoanuts which he and Jane husked for her father, and between the cooling milk inside and the firm white meat of the nut itself, they managed to stay their hunger.

Then Jane took the ape's hand and he led the way in the direction he thought Tarzan had taken, while the Professor followed with many misgivings.

If he had known how near Rokoff and Gernot were, he would have been still more unhappy. The two rascals were only a short distance off, cosily seated under the shadow of some dwarf trees. They had breakfast and with lighted cigaretts were discussing prospects ahead of them.

"We haven't had one bit of luck since the sinking of the Lady Alice," remarked Rokoff morosely. "Clayton's disappeared, God knows where— probably lions got him. The girl keeps escaping us—our expedition is shot to hell—and we have neither ivory nor the gold of Opar—"

"Don't forget that we have lost the map of Opar also, mon ami, while you are adding up our calamities here," put in Gernot dryly. "You are a cheerful companion, I must say."

"Well, who wouldn't be?" Rokoff kept on. "Here you and I might be waking up in our cosy apartment on the rue de la Paix, just resting from a night along the Boulevards with the bright lights and the pretty girls—and what do we see here instead of beautiful faces—monkeys! Pah!" He flung a stone at an ugly ringtail babboon who had swung down to investigate where the pungent tobacco smoke came from.

"Well—" Gernot supplemented, twisting his little black moustache, "you are in effect quite right. As for myself, the only wild things I like are what an American friend of mine used to call wild women—and one does not find them anywhere else in the world like in Paris."

"And that's why I say," put in Rokoff, "now that we have the formula, let's beat it toward where Raoul is waiting with the airplane and let the girl go."

"Softly, my friend," put in Gernot. "Do you despise money so much, is gold so little to you? On the girl's shoulder lies the map of Opar and it would be so easy to take all that wonderful treasure you have described to me so eloquently from those ignorant dwarfs."

Rokoff was about to answer him when the words were cut right out of his mouth, for with a rushing crash through the underbrush a great brack-maned lion sprang between them, knocking both men flat as he ran on and, as Rokoff started to jump to his feet, another lion which was pursuing the first almost ran over him. The two men hastily fled from the spot without finishing their conversation.

Meantime Og, the friendly ape, had led Jane and the Professor almost to the same place. Warned by the scent of the lion, Og made frantic sounds expressive of fear and raced further into the underbrush, dragging Jane with him. The Professor most foolishly made for a small tree directly in the path of the beast and, as he was only able to get up a very little way in its small branches for fear they would give way under him, the lion was able to jump up at him and occasionally stick a claw in his flapping coat tails whereupon the dignified scientist's cries of terror re-echoed through the forest.

Tarzan had wandered in search of Rokoff until he despaired of finding him, when a familiar trumpeting caused him to shout joyfully "Tantor!"

The huge beast was in a bad humor; he was walking through a stretch of grass which had small prickly vines in it and they pierced even through his thick skin and caused him intense discomfort, he therefore did not hurry toward his human friend as usual but uttered several peevish cries and grunts to inform Tarzan that he was seriously uncomfortable over something.

Tarzan swung himself down from the branches alongside of the big elephant and, raising first one foot and then the other, he soon relieved him of all the thorns, some of which had even lodged in the tender flesh between his great toes.

Tantor nuzzled him affectionately with his trunk and lifted him on his broad back, so in this manner the two friends swung through the forest until Tarzan's keen ears detected the frantic cries of the Professor. He gave Tantor the signal to lower him and came creeping cautiously through the underbrush in the direction from whence the sounds came.

But he was not the only one who was attracted by Professor Porter's cries for help unfortunately. Gernot and Rokoff also hastened to the spot for they knew that Jane was with her father.

"Yes, we must get Jane Porter," Rokoff had agreed. "With the gold of Opar in our hands we shall be able to make better use of the gas. Who knows we may be the rulers of Soviet Russia, and then of the world!"

But Gernot shook his head with annoyance. "All will be well if we don't run across Tarzan," he said. "This mad man is getting on my nerves. We can't beat him. When we get the girl we'd better hurry to the desert, get a new expedition and start for Opar at once!"

As he finished this statement, they arrived within sight of the clearing where the lion was jumping up and down frantically trying to reach the Professor in the little tree while Og held Jane in the crouch of a larger one a little further off.

It so happened that Gernot had to pass under that very tree and the bull ape, snarling horribly in his rage, dropped upon him with bared teeth and outstretched crushing arms. But Rokoff, who was right behind him, laid Og low with a shot from his revolver.

With a cry of savage triumph he dragged Jane from the branches and subdued her struggles with the help of Gernot.

It was at this point that Tarzan appeared

and started in hot pursuit of the trio. The way lay toward two high cliffs between which flowed a branch of the same stream they had forded during the fire. Up one of these steep cliffs Gernot hastened with the girl, while Rokoff and Tarzan brought up the rear. Without using their usual forethought and caution, Tarzan flung himself on the Frenchman with such violence that he and the girl lost their balance and fell over the edge into the water.

There was only one thing to do. Tarzan dived after Jane and brought her to the surface, just as she was going down for the second time. She was an excellent swimmer but she had struck her head in the sudden involuntary dive and was dizzy and almost unconscious. Tarzan swam with her to the other bank and laid her on the grass of the opposite cliff. Then, seeing no signs of Gernot in the swiftly flowing waters, he swam back to the other shore and, with a grim tightening of his lips, sprang up the grassy slope leading to the edge of the other cliff where Rokoff stood absorbed in watching for signs of his comrade.

Tarzan did not waste a minute in useless parlay but sprang like a panther on the Russian's back and bore him to the earth.

The two men rolled over and over, cursing and snarling like two wild beasts, while Jane, on the opposite bank watched and prayed with her heart almost suffocating her by its rapid beats. She feared tremendously for Tarzan who was under Rokoff and with his head almost at the very edge of the cliff over which Rokoff was working him inch by inch as he pressed with all his strength against the giant's throat.

But all at once the big form of Tarzan gathered itself up with a spring, at the same moment still holding the surprised Rokoff in his mighty grip he gave the Russian's body a sudden swing upwards and before even Jane realized it, he threw him clear over his shoulder down into the river.

But as Tarzan straightened from this almost superhuman effort and tried to get the breath back into his lungs, there was a swift spring from something tawny which sped like an arrow from the bushes behind him, and a huge lioness bore him down with her into the rushing waters below.

CHAPTER X

THE SIMOON

Jane gave a shriek of horror as she saw the lion spring on Tarzan and knock him over the cliff into the swift current below. For a moment she could perceive nothing and then his head and massive shoulders were seen making their way swiftly toward the shore and the lion presently emerged, swimming like the great cat he was, in fear and in rage at the element he so detested.

So silent was the girl in watching whether her lover reached safety that she did not notice footsteps behind her, until, all of a sudden, she found herself gripped from behind and heard the mocking voice of Gernot saying:

"Ah, I have you again, Mademoiselle."

He had been swimming mostly under water and had landed further down the stream where Tarzan could not see him stealthily make his way back of the girl to capture her. In a minute he was rejoined by Rokoff, who also was an excellent swimmer and who had escaped with the money belt.

The girl put up a desperate struggle. She not only did not wish to be captured but she wanted to see what had become of Tarzan. But she was entirely helpless in the grasp of the two men and they half dragged, half carried her away with them. When they were a short distance away from the bank they paused for a moment to take counsel and then they heard faintly borne on the breeze the voice of Tarzan raised in the call of death and of victory.

"He is then alive!" gasped Gernot.

"Yes, my friend," answered his partner, "and it is we who will not be alive if we do not make haste to find our airplane and get far away from here!"

Gernot shrugged his shoulders. "Tarzan has killed the last of our men. We must return to the desert and secure a new expedition before we can go on to Opar," he agreed.

They made what haste they could, dragging the unwilling Jane toward the spot where they had left their plane. Their path lay through the untrodden jungle and at every step either one of them was forced to hack away vines and oftentime thorny undergrowth, while the other held Jane, who was ready to run away and hide herself in the thickest part of the forest rather than trust herself with these men.

Finally they swung into a trail which they recognized as the one which they had trodden before and, by sunrise of the next morning, they found themselves on the edge of the desert looking at the remains of a camp from which every sign of life had departed.

A pot swung cold and empty between its sticks over the burnt embers of a dead fire. An old cast off coat lay on the ground. These were the only signs that a human being had ever been there. Gernot swore viciously. Rokoff, being of a calmer frame of mind, investigated and found a note fastened to a young tree. It was from the mechanic left in charge of their airplane, and read as follows:

"Food all gone. You stayed a week too long. Shall return with provisions.   Raoul."

"Let us find a place of safety and wait the return of the plane," the Frenchman suggested.

"Not this close to Tarzan," answered Rokoff. "That man can scent us a mile. He is like a bloodhound. I'm in favor of hitting out across the desert and meeting some tribe."

After thinking about it a bit the other agreed with him and, leaving a note for Raoul, they set out across the sands.

In the meantime Professor Porter was still marooned in his tree with an angry lion making jumps and stabs at him with its sharp claws. As it grew dark the lion grew discouraged and wandered off to find easier prey, but the professor stayed shivering with fear in the branches of the small tree until morning, which is the wisest thing he could have done for the prowlers of the forest would certainly have put an end to him if he had set foot on the ground. As it was, he repeatedly saw greenish eyes shining in the darkness, heard the pad of the big cat's feet as leopard and lion passed right under the tree and once he heard a lion spring with a roar on some poor little member of the deer family, and then heard him quarreling with his mate over the carcass. It was not a night for a timid man, and the professor could never by any stretch of the imagination have been called a hero.

Towards dawn he dropped off into a fitful doze and he awoke champed and almost falling out of the tree, but with the blessed sunshine beating on his face and the bull ape underneath the tree calling and making signs to him.

The professor was so glad to see a friendly face, whether that of a human or an animal, that he almost sprained his ankle in his haste to come down out of the tree.

With many signs the ape indicated that he was to follow him as he led the way first to a little spring where the man was able to drink and refresh himself, and then through the forest with a rapid shambling gait which Jane's father found it hard to follow. They came upon Tantor standing in the shelter of some trees pulling at their foliage. When he saw the bull ape he trumpeted in friendly greeting and Og, rubbing his hairy face against his trunk, spoke to him in the language of the jungle:

"Tantor, I am going to put this man on your back—take care of him for he is the father of the mate of our big Tarmangani chief."

The elephant knelt that Professor Porter might mount him more easily and then, flapping his big ears as a sign he was content, he swung along through the jungle with his charge comfortably seated on his back.

Then the faithful ape set out to find Tarzan and from the tree tops he spied him following the scent of trail of his two enemies. The faithful animal swung rapidly through the branches and soon rejoined his master, just as the latter came to the edge of the desert where the remains of Raoul's camp stood.

Like his predecessors, Tarzan looked for some sign and presently he found it in the answer to Raoul's note written by Gernot and fastened to the same tree.

"Return across the desert and pick us up, we are heading for Sagamore."

Tarzan's grim laugh reechoed through the lonely spot. "Thanks for your information!" he bowed ironically and tore the bit of paper into fragments which in turn he buried in the sand.

"And now Og," he said to the bull ape, "you

must return to the jungle, my friend, as I am taking a long trip across the desert."

The ape said nothing but fell back a few steps until Tarzan was almost out of sight, and then the faithful animal followed him swiftly across the sands.

Gernot and Rokoff had started for Sagarone with a very good reason. The map of Opar had disappeared from Jane's back, thanks to the treatment Tarzan had given it every day, and neither one of the rascals could make out a single one of its outlines.

"Gone!" Rokoff ejaculated with an oath, but Gernot replied, "Be patient, my friend, all is not yet lost. Hagar, the mystic will apply a lotion that will bring the scar to sight once we get to Sagarone."

And so, both for men to form a new expedition and because they needed the services of the beggar Hagar, they headed for the little Arab town.

In Sagarone Hagar outwardly lived the life of a beggar but used his calling of asker of alms and mystic to cloak darker transactions which brought in far more money such as harboring criminals, receiving stolen goods, arranging intrigues and even conniving at murder and abduction.

He was sitting on the steps of a mosque in the sun when two ragged and footsore men stood before him. Scenting possible rivals, Hagar raised the patch from a presumably blind eye and attacked them vigorously with his cane, only to be interrupted by a voice he knew, that of Gernot. He recognized his former generous patron under the mask of dirt and rags, not to speak of a tangled and matted beard.

"What can I do for you, Excellency," he stammered, bowing and scraping very low. "And is the maiden for sale?"

"Not at present, at least," answered the Russian. "What we want of you, O wise one, is simple. It consists merely in bringing back some mystic signs we imprinted on her back."

Hagar chuckled and bowed once more deeply. "All the poor knowledge that Allah has placed at my disposal shall be at your command," he agreed, "but my price for this—"

"Never mind your price," snapped Gernot, "Do as we ask and we'll have all the gold in the world to make you rich. Come rascal, move your feet and take us to your lodgings!"

In a few minutes they were securely hidden in Hagar's lodgings down an obscure alley. Shabby though the entrance was, the interior belied it. Costly rugs hung on the walls and decorated the floors, gold and silver plate and ornaments stolen from caravans by the robber bands to which he belonged were scattered around with studied carelessness. Hagar led Jane to a divan and bared the leopard skin from her shoulder.

He pursed his lips and nodded his grey head. "Yes, I can bring it back for a consideration—" he began, looking at the faint remaining marks of the map.

Gernot interrupted him impatiently. "I tell you fool that you will be rich beyond the dreams of avarice if you will but help us with this."

The beggar drew a small vial from a chest of carved and inlaid precious wood and applied a few drops of its contents to the delicate skin of Jane's shoulder. It burned like fire and strange mottlings and marks appeared on it.

Hagar turned to the two men and gave the bottle into Gernot's hands.

"Retain that bottle of blue," said he. "Within the hour the map will appear. Should you require it again the contents of that bottle will bring it to view."

Rokoff became restless at the wait. "Leave the bottle with me," he said to Gernot, "and go to the coffee house. See if any of Sheik Ben Ali's men are there. If so bring them here and see if there is not a barber. I want to look my best when I meet Queen La."

Gernot, who was not unwilling to freshen up himself, departed in the direction of the bazaar, leaving Rokoff to wait impatiently the action of the lotion. Slowly the lines began to appear and Rokoff hastened the action with another application of the fluid. Quite a bit within the appointed time the map began to appear clearly and distinctly soon it was all there and Rokoff set to work copying it feverishly.

He had barely finished when the door opened and Gernot coquettishly and fastidiously barbered, and wearing a clean suit of white duck appeared.

"I have done all your errands," the Frenchman answered. "The barber awaits you, he is even now heating your bath and while you take it and are shaved I shall stay and guard the girl."

Rokoff gladly made his exit and Gernot stood with his back against the closed door twisting his little black moustache.

There was a sob from Jane and she desperately began to appeal to this man who seemed to her less of a brute than the other, to protect her, save her, and set her free.

Gernot's answer was to walk over to the

divan and tear the leopard skin once more from her shoulder—then he, too, eagerly seized pencil and paper and eagerly copied the map of Opar.

Then disdainfully tapping the leopard skin with the point of one highly polished finger nail, he commanded her to change her nether clothes.

There is a chest here of women's fripperies," said the Frenchman. "Take what you will to make yourself beautiful and be quick about it." He tossed her a Turkish costume, spangled trousers, golden slippers and everything to go with them— clothes belonging to women who had met Hagar— and disappeared.

Jane, who did not dare to refuse him, begged him to turn away while she dressed, and he looked out of the window down on the busy square below. Hiding herself behind the curtains of the dais, she pulled on the Turkish girl's costume and soon stood before him looking as lovely as any harem rose.

As Gernot turned from his contemplation of the market place to observe her, he drew in his breath sharply with admiration, his eyes glowed with an unholy light as he advanced toward her. Jane realized then what danger she was in and she dodged him adroitly, making him advance some distance into the middle of the room, when she suddenly made a rush for the open window and, without even stopping to look where she was going, she jumped over the low balcony railing into the street below.

While Gernot and Rokoff were continuing in their evil ways, Tarzan and the bull ape were wandering half crazed with thirst across the sands. They were utterly lost and fell into the hands of Yosoff's outlaw band which lay in wait for a rich pearl caravan. Believing that Tarzan was the advance guard of the caravan, the cruel bandit tortured him to make him tell where it was. He dripped fresh, cool water near him on the ground and would not let the weakened man get near it.

In vain Tarzan repeated, "I know nothing of a caravan. I am looking for two men carrying a girl toward Sagarone."

The outlaw answered, "you heathen swine, before Allah receives this day's sun the vultures will be feasting upon you."

But all Tarzan could answer through stiffening lips was "I know nothing of the caravan."

"So be it!" exclaimed the chief, exasperated. "Bring the wild steed and bind this liar to his back—thus shall he be carried back bound to his heathen lands."

In vain Tarzan struggled, he was weak and spent. They bound him to the back of a fiery Arab horse that had never known the touch of man before. A great wind had risen in the meantime, and was blowing little eddies of sand about the horse's feet and into the men's eyes as they were seeing to the fastenings. The sky became a lurid yellow and, with a shriek like that of a departed soul, one of the sudden storms, only to be found on the great desert, descended upon them.

"The Simoon!" shouted the chief to his followers. "Save yourselves!" With a slash of his rawhide whip he sent the untamed stallion and the helpless man on its back flying into the gathering darkness of the sand-swept desert.

CHAPTER XI

THE SLAVE MARKET

The maddened stallion had never felt anything tied to him before, least of all a man. He reared once under the lash of the Arab and then plunged, with the helpless Tarzan on his back, right into the teeth of the sandstorm.

Tarzan, who was tied with his face against the animal's hide, thus had his eyes and nose protected from the flying sand, but not so the horse. Particles of it filled his sensitive nostrils and entered his inflamed eyes, still further maddening him. He ended by running blindly in circles and then stumbled and fell. He almost immediately scrambled to his feet and started on more madly than before, but Tarzan had felt something give way and, just as the animal gathered himself for a fresh burst of speed, the entire rope parted and he was thrown down the side of a sand bank while the stallion galloped away more frightened than ever.

The man lay there completely exhausted and not a little stunned. He was protected from the greatest fury of the storm and presently it died down with the same suddenness that it began. He then discovered that it was possible to work off the ravelling cord little by little until finally he was free, although sorely bruised and bleeding. His thirst was almost unbearable and he thought he was the victim of another mirage when he saw what appeared to be the bull ape crawling down the sand bank bearing with utmost care a water skin.

But in this he was mistaken. The faithful ape had prowled around the ruins of the Arab camp until he found the goatskin where the water was kept. Then he shambled across the sands following the hoof marks of the stallion, until he arrived in time to save his master's life. As the blessed trickle of water passed down his parched throat, Tarzan felt renewed life in his veins, and with it the desire to outwit his enemies.

"And now for a horse!" he exclaimed, and almost as if by magic one appeared. It was ridden by an Arab, however, and who was armed and was about to pass within a short distance of him.

Seizing the longest piece of rope, Tarzan made a lasso of it and it whistled around the arms of the unsuspecting desert rider. Before he ever knew what struck him, he was dragged from the horse's back and half choked in the sand. When he came to sufficiently to open his eyes Tarzan had his silver mounted pistols, and was ordering him in the native form of French to make himself scarce.

The horse willingly came to Tarzan, as all animals did, and springing in the saddle he swung the ape up behind him and they were both off like a streak in the direction of Sagarone.

In Sagarone itself things were not well. Rokoff, standing outside the barber shop, resplendent in fresh linen and a shave, saw Jane leap from the window and promptly seized her. He half carried, half dragged her upstairs into Hagar's room and all the while he was so angry he could hardly see, for he more than suspected treachery on Gernot's part for the first time.

The two friends had bitter words and from words came to blows. Hagar interfered with his oily, smooth voice:

"Come, come, gentlemen!" he purred, but there was menace in the tones. "You must be quiet! I love peace!"

Rokoff's answer was to draw his revolver on Gernot, but quicker than any panther's movement was Hagar as he snatched it from him and covering the Frenchman he commanded him to give up his weapon likewise. He then, with many chuckles, emptied both of their cartridges and remarked:

"As soon as you are friendly messieurs, I shall return you these little pellets of death!"

The two men, therefore, had to take it out in talk while Hagar, hearing a noise on the stairway, went out to investigate.

He found Sheik Ben Ali in a very ugly and disappointed frame of mind. To Hagar's eager inquiries about the pearl caravan, the bandit returned impatiently:

"We had to return to town as fast as we could to seek a place of safety. The pearl caravan passed under guard of two hundred French."

Hagar clicked his tongue sharply against his teeth and answered: "Allah is great! It would have been madness to have attacked it!"

The sheik gave a disgusted and discouraged shake of the head. He had banked greatly on the capture of the caravan.

"Rokoff the Nihilist is here," ventured Hagar more hopefully, "with the news of a great fortune in gold half a moon's travel southward."

"He wants men and guns then? It is well. I shall let have them and will go with him—but when we get the gold—well, we don't need him to help us spend it?"

Ben Ali's smile was evil as he motioned that

Hagar should take him upstairs and introduce him to the strangers.

The beggar pushed open the door of the room where Rokoff and Gernot still stood apart glaring at each other.

"Gentlemen, here is Ben Ali," he said. "He can furnish you with the men for your expedition if you come to terms."

The three men eagerly drew together in a little group. Hagar let his eyes wander to where the girl crouched, in the window seat, trembling with fear. He allowed a benevolent smile to come over his oily face. It was like a miracle, a ray of light in a dark dungeon to poor Jane. He would help her. Her trembling lips formed a little pale smile in return, her beautiful dark eyes pleaded with all her heart in them.

Hagar rubbed his hands with satisfaction. What a price she would bring in the slave market! He smiled back at her paternally, reassuringly and, with one eye on the group of arguing men, counselled caution with his finger on his lip.

Gernot with eyes rolled heavenward was repeating what Rokoff had told him of the comeliness of the women of the tribe of Opar.

Ben Ali interrupted him impatiently:

"Never mind the beauty of the women monsieur," he cried. "What share do I get of this gold?"

Gernot came back to earth and his little eyes narrowed with greed. "You and your men receive one—third of the loot, the remainder shall be ours," he answered.

The Sheik laughed unpleasantly and shook his head. "By the prophet, do you men think me a fool that I should risk my men for that!" he exclaimed. "Come, monsieur, think again! Time presses!"

The argument was resumed angrily.

Hagar tiptoed to the door and motioned to the girl: Together they crept out while the men were deep in their discussion. Throwing his mantle around her so that none should observe her beauty, Hagar drew her down the crooked street and, through devious and winding ways, until they reached the public square where the slave market was being held that day.

The auctioneer willingly left his post and descended to where Hagar held by the wrist the girl who, too late, realized why he had rescued her. She begged and pleaded with him, she even knelt at his feet. He only laughed at her and departed, clinking his little bag of gold while she was promptly raised to the block. As Hagar turned the corner he heard the voices of the crowd raised in wild bidding for her beauty.

Meanwhile, back in the room they had discovered that she was missing.

"Hagar is gone also," cried the jealous Rokoff. Ben Ali came as near an open laugh as his desert breeding would allow him.

"Calm yourself," he sneered. "Hagar is not your rival. The slave market is open today and he has probably taken her there and sold her!"

"Get her back for me and you can name your price!" cried Rokoff wildly.

The sheik ran down the steps and sprang to his horse's back. He rode down the narrow street like the wind, and, past the slave block he swooped downward from his saddle with unfailing aim and lifted the girl up in front of him, without losing a single jot of speed. He was pursued by a shower of stones and maledictions from the auctioneer and the crowd of bidders.

When he arrived at the house again he picked Jane up in his arms as if she had been a feather and deposited her in the room where Gernot and Rokoff were waiting.

"Here is your captive, messieurs. I wish you joy of her!" he exclaimed. "I would not have her in my harem for she fought like a wild cat, and I think her tongue must be as sharp as her nails."

He smiled mockingly as he rearranged the folds of his mantle and turban.

There was a creak of the door and the face of Hagar anxiously peered through the crack. Rokoff, with an oath, shot out one of his long arms and dragged the beggar in.

"Dog," he snarled. "What do you mean by double crossing me?"

"Softly! Softly!" whined Hagar, but with an ominous glitter in his eyes. "I needed the money."

Ben Ali laughed. Rokoff gave one look at the lean face of the sheik, at Hagar's evil look, and decided to let the matter drop.

"Well—take care what you do, that's all! I have my eye on you," he growled.

The girl had returned to her post by the window and Rokoff drew her farther from the others into the recess.

"Jane," he began. "Why will you persist in hating me when I love you with my whole heart? You are one against many and you will have to give up all idea of Tarzan. He is dead now without a doubt for the sheik tells me he bound him to the back of an untamed horse and sent him out into the desert during a sandstorm to die of thirst. No man can escape a fate like that even if he be a Tarzan. You will forget him in my arms and be both rich and happy. Come, be a sensible girl and do the right thing by me!"

Jane strained away from him as far as she could, and her eyes flashed the scorn she could hardly put into words.

"Do me the favor of keeping your love making for the kind of woman you are used to giving it to," she cried. "I despise you!"

Rokoff smoothed his little mustache with a twirl of his big hand. "You will not hate me, my dear, when I cover you with diamonds," he observed fatuously.

Jane grew, if possible, paler with indignation. "Rather than submit to your kind of love I would kill myself!" she sobbed with tears in her eyes.

The mocking laughter of Gernot, who enjoyed Rokoff's discomfiture, here interrupted their conversation.

The men who were thus calmly plotting their villainy little realized that their dreaded enemy, Tarzan, was even then entering the town. He stopped at a shabby little inn on the outskirts of town where he left his horse and the faithful bull ape and on foot, he crept into the bazaar to hear what news he might.

There he found the greatest topic of conversation was how Sheik Ben Ali had violated all the rules of the slave market by stealing the beautiful white captive, in which Tarzan had no difficulty in recognizing Jane.

"Poor little girl, what has become of her by this time?" thought the anguished Tarzan, and he only waited to hear the place where the sheik had taken her.

The crowd was evidently afraid of mobbing the house of Hagar, which was well known and feared on account of the many murders and mysterious disappearances which had taken place within its walls.

Finally, using some of the gold he had taken from the lassoed Arab, Tarzan bribed a small boy to show his the way. The youngster promptly fled as soon as he had collected his reward, and Tarzan stationed himself in an arched doorway opposite, which was dark enough to partly conceal him.

A hand overhead dropped a rose at his feet and he looked up eagerly, but a swarthy pair of eyes behind a spangled veil which framed the lower half of a plump face did not deceive him into thinking it was blue eyed Jane.

He saw lights behind the lattice of the house opposite—he even heard voices—and all of a sudden he saw the slender form of his beloved back away, as if from some one, and stand clearly outlined against the light and the window. With a prayer that she might turn Tarzan flipped a pebble against the colored glass.

At the slight tinkling sound, Jane started and looking into the street, she saw outlined in the doorway opposite, the beloved figure of Tarzan.

With a gesture of caution toward the part of the room he could not see, she put her hand to her lips and then stretched it out toward him in a gesture in which all the love and the longing in the world were expressed.

Tarzan made a swift dash across the street, aided by the growing dusk, and began to climb the side of the house, clinging to the ornamentations and the uneven stones. The luck of the lovers was with him, for he swung himself over the sill and into the room before the sleepy Arab on guard had time to dash upstairs and report his coming.

With a mighty war cry, Tarzan hurled himself on Gernot and Rokoff. He even scorned to use his revolver. He seized and threw them against the wall, choking them and beating them until they cried aloud for mercy. The sheik, at first taken aback by his sudden entrance, started to draw his revolver, but was silenced by a swift blow on the temple dealt with a heavily inlaid stool.

Gernot and Rokoff, whose guns had been emptied by Hagar, lay stunned and bleeding and the beggar himself ran shrieking down the stairs trying to reach the rest of the Arabs.

"Come quickly, oh come quickly," he besought them. "There is a madman upstairs killing your master!"

Just as he was about to turn back, accompanied by three or four of the bandits, Tarzan appeared half way down the stairs with the girl in his arms.

For Hagar to act was the work of a second. He almost threw himself across the room until he reached and pressed down a hidden lever. The entire stairway appeared to buckle up, double itself, turn over with its living freight and hurl them into the dungeons deep down beneath the opened flooring of the house.

CHAPTER XII

DYNAMITE TRAIL

When Hagar touched the spring which controlled the trick stairway and it doubled up hurling Tarzan and his sweetheart Jane into the cellar, the beggar gave vent to one of his evil cackles of laughter.

"They'll not bother me any more!" Hagar chuckled. "And now to make a little more money."

He waddled upstairs where he found Gernot, Rokoff and Ben Ali stretched out on the floor nursing aching heads and many bruises.

With hypocritical expressions of sympathy Hagar aided them to rise and bandage their injuries.

"Your prisoners are safe in my cellar, gentlemen," he assured them, much to their joy, and he led them to where they could see Tarzan and the girl in the cellar dungeon.

The joy of the three conspirators however somewhat dampened by the old plotter's next remark:

"The birds are in my cage now. Pay high and join them. Refuse and you can stay where you are!"

"For heaven's sake, pay him!" groaned Rokoff. "Tarzan has all my money in the belt containing the formula."

With many curses Gernot dug down into the secret pockets of his khaki suit and brought forth gold and banknotes for the greedy hands of Hagar. The latter, true to his word, pressed the spring which brought the stairway back into place and the three rascals descended to work fresh mischief upon their helpless captives.

Unfortunately for their plans, Tarzan had not been inactive. After the first shock of the fall, and when he had found that neither he nor Jane was more than badly shaken up, he had carefully explored the cellar and found a high grated window which looked out on the alley back of Hagar's house. The iron bars which guarded this would have been far too heavy for any ordinary man, but Tarzan had the strength of the savage apes among whom he had been bred.

He laughed with pleasure when he saw only four stanchions for him to bend.

"Watch around the corner of this pillar and tell me if you hear some one coming. I'll make short work of this," he told Jane.

He had thrust out one powerful arm to take a firmer hold on the first bar, when he heard a whimper of joy and the faithful ape, who had been prowling around the house trying to find an entrance, rubbed his muzzle against his master's hand.

"Your horse is here, too, Oh great Tarmangani," chattered the ape. "I thought you might come to no good here in the haunts of men and so might need a trusty steed at hand."

Tarzan patted the ape's hand and bent to the work of pulling out the bars. In the time the others took to talk things over upstairs and to pay Hagar his blood money the bars were all out. When Jane reported that their enemies were coming down the stairs, the lovers just had the necessary minutes to make their escape through the opened window.

When Rokoff and Gernot cautiously

advanced into the semi-darkness of the cellar it was to find it empty, the clatter of hoofs growing fainter down the village street told them the truth, and the Arab guards gave them the additional information that Tarzan and the girl had headed straight for the governor's house.

This was bad news for the trio. Tarzan had the incriminating sheepskin which, submitted first to heat and then wet, would reveal handwriting which would cost them their lives or at least long imprisonment.

Ben Ali was the first to recover his assurance.

"Fortunately Suzette is maid in his Excellency's house," he remarked, "and while Suzette may take her wages from him she takes her orders from me."

It was indeed by that smiling little French maid that Tarzan and Jane were admitted to the governor's house.

They were not kept waiting but were immediately ushered into his presence for he had heard of Tarzan and had long wished to meet him. After the introductions were over and Suzette still hung around, Tarzan made signs to the governor that he wished to be alone.

His Excellency remarked graciously, "Perhaps madame would like to be refreshed."

Upon Jane's signifying her willingness, he ordered Suzette to take her to his daughter's apartments. As soon as the wily maid left the room she returned downstairs and ran lightly across the lawn to where she saw an Arab leaning with apparent laziness against the iron gate.

"Quick, go to your master, Ben Ali, and tell him Tarzan is closeted with the governor, and will let no one hear what he is saying," Suzette gasped.

The Arab ran on this errand at top speed, and delivered it much to the dismay of Gernot and Rokoff.

"We must get that parchment back," they cried to Hagar. "Can't you help us any way at all?"

Hagar shrugged his hunched shoulders and reached down into the pouch he wore beneath his rags.

"Gentlemen," he whined, "I happen to have here, just by chance, a powder which might do the trick. It is contained in a sort of bomb. When you throw it, it explodes and the suffocating gases render unconscious all in the immediate vicinity."

Rokoff and Gernot simultaneously stretched out their hands. "The very thing!" they both cried.

But Hagar drew the gift away. "For a consideration," he chuckled, as he tapped his money bag.

With curses the pair gave him the price he asked, and seizing the powder, they ran to the governor's house as fast as their feet would carry them.

Tarzan and the Governor had just finished reading the parchment and the official had thanked Tarzan in the name of France for the service he had rendered that country as its secret agent, when there was knocking at the door.

"We had best put this in the safe," remarked the governor. As the two men stood in front of the combination, the door was suddenly burst open in defiance of its flimsy lock. Before either of them could make a move something was thrown in their direction, after which they fell on their faces and remembered nothing.

As they lay there unconscious, Gernot and Rokoff, who had been admitted by Suzette, robbed

117

them of the precious parchment and ran from the house carrying Jane with them.

When Tarzan came back to his senses and managed to drag the Governor out into the open air he found Suzette limp and dishevelled lying where she had placed herself across the entrance and she moaned that Mademoiselle had been stolen from her and taken away in the direction of the South.

Tarzan believed her, and would have rushed away in the opposite direction from that taken by his sweetheart, but he ran across the bull ape, who told him the truth.

"They went in the direction where the beggar man is going," cried the faithful animal in ape language and Tarzan, who understood everything he said perfectly, soon overtook Hagar and gave that worthy a choking and a beating that he remembered for many a day.

"Where are they headed for?" growled Tarzan. "Answer, dog!"

As soon as he could get enough breath Hagar anxiously tried to placate this madman who was a giant for strength.

For once in his life, such was his fright, he spoke the entire truth:

"I—I don't know where it is, O mighty one," he quavered. "I am only a poor beggar, but I heard them say, 'Let us go on to Opar.'"

"You have saved your worthless life by telling me that," Tarzan answered, flinging him to the ground. "Now be wise and get out of my sight and never re-enter it."

Hagar did not waste any time in putting distance between himself and his enemy. Tarzan, without a moment's delay, set out in the direction of Opar.

He secured a lift from a caravan which led him in safety across the sands and once he was set down from the camel's back on the edge of the forest, he took to the trees as soon as possible and swung from one branch to the other whenever possible to avoid being seen by anyone who might report his presence to his enemies, for he wished to surprise them utterly. In this manner he arrived at the very spot where they had pitched their tents not far from the volcano and the hidden city of the dwarfs of Opar.

There was bitterness and recrimination in the camp of the three one time friends. Jane was the cause of it. They had fastened her securely to a tree and each one of the adventurers tried to steal up to her and enter into conversation with her whenever possible. And besides, Gernot, for purposes of his own was sowing the seeds of hatred against Rokoff in Ben Ali's mind and the Arab had already determined that before the gold of Opar was divided there would be one less of them to share it.

At the moment when Tarzan looked down upon the camp, Rokoff was standing near Jane whispering into her ear, but Jane indignantly repulsed his love making.

"You can place bonds on my arms," the girl answered him proudly, "but you can not make me forget Tarzan. He will follow me and he will rescue me and punish you, so leave me alone. You are wasting your time."

Rokoff flushed with annoyance both at her words and at the laughter of the other two who were looking on and who knew from the girl's frowns that she was repulsing him.

He swung away from her, muttering. "When you decide to be nice to me, I'll release you!"

"Og," commanded Tarzan, to the faithful bull ape, who crouched by his side among the branches, "Go and warn the people of Opar, your friends, that these bandits are about to attack them. I'll stay here and listen to what these fools have to say."

The ape bounded away through the trees and Tarzan, in his anxiety to hear more, drew a little nearer.

He saw Ben Ali broil a tender piece of venison over the fire and advance toward the girl. Jane, who was very hungry, accepted it with gratitude, but Rokoff flung himself on the tall Arab and shook him.

"Keep your place," the big Russian yelled, almost beside himself with jealousy and anger. "Any more interference and I'll leave you for the buzzards!"

Gernot crept up to where Ben Ali had angrily retreated. "You see, sheik, how he insults a man of your standing!" he purred. "We shall really have to get rid of him."

The sheik looked up moodily and the sunlight fell directly on Tarzan's figure standing in a crotch of the branches almost directly overhead.

Ben Ali started and pointed him out to Gernot before he swiftly disappeared. "The wild man of the jungle is in the trees nearby!" he exclaimed.

Gernot saw his opportunity of getting even with Rokoff.

"Yes, and as long as the girl is our prisoner he will trail us!" he answered. To himself, he added, "I can even up my score with Rokoff by demanding that he leave her here."

"If we are to get the gold she certainly is in our way," agreed Ben Ali.

"Well, let us put Tarzan off our trail by leaving the girl and let us get on our way to Opar immediately!" suggested Gernot.

Rokoff came up at this moment and the other two put the plan to him so forcibly that he had no choice but agree.

"But she must be left safe and sound, so I may find her on my return," he stipulated.

"My friend," the Arab said, "she shall be guarded so safe and high that neither man nor beast can reach her. Monsieur Gernot here plans to place her in the wicker look-out basket which we suspend from a tree for our sentinels. She shall be placed at the summit of a tall palm from which all branches have been removed. She will not be able to climb down, nor will anyone be able to climb up because we shall mine the base of it with sticks of dynamite."

Rokoff was forced to admit that the plan sounded safe enough and accordingly he himself led Jane into the basket which had been filled with provisions and with a water skin, and he lifted the girl up to her wicker prison.

"I am going to leave you in this look-out tower with food and water, and when I return from Opar my love shall be yours," he told her.

Ben Ali and Gernot laughted to themselves. "When he returns from Opar!" they mocked under their breaths.

At a signal the Arabs pulled on the ropes and the basket was hoisted to the top of the tree and made fast.

The Arabs were standing for one last look at their work before leaving, when they saw Tarzan spring to the top of the tree nearest Jane. The girl saw him too and held out her arms to him with a gesture of frantic appeal. Tarzan seized his trusty rope, looped it over the branches of his tree and swung far out over the basket which held his sweetheart. Nicely calculating the distance he dropped right into it and clasped her to his heart.

Rokoff's passion rose up and choked him.

"Fire!" he commanded the Arabs, pointing to the base of the tree where the dynamite was. They raised their guns to their shoulders and obeyed.

There was a terrific explosion, dirt and rocks were thrown into the air and the basket containing Jane and Tarzan came crashing to the ground.

CHAPTER XIII

THE JUNGLE'S PREY

To Jane, crouching in her basket on the top of the tall palm, frightened almost to death and hopelessly praying for deliverance, the sight of Tarzan in the tree nearest to her seemed almost like a vision born of her shattered nerves. But when she stretched out her arms to him and cried his name and he answered, she knew God had indeed heard her prayer.

Tarzan flung his trusty rope over the branches and swung far out over her watch tower prison. On the backward swing, which he made the backward swing, which he nicely calculated the distance and dropped into the basket at her side and then, hardly had her arms found their way around his neck, when she heard the voice of Rokoff hoarse with jealousy and passion.

"Fire," he commanded the Arabs, and she remembered how the base of her tree was mined—with dynamite.

There was a blinding flash and a roar that shook the earth and she felt herself and Tarzan falling as the basket and the palm tree lurched downward to their ruin.

She closed her eyes and clung to him, but she forgot the end of his trusty rope which he still wore fastened around his waist. The other loop was firmly fastened to the branches from which he had swung to her rescue. Tarzan took a leap far out from the falling basket just a second before it struck the ground and, still holding his sweetheart close to him with one arm, he reached for the foliage of the tree he had just left behind and so pulled them both to safety.

It all had happened so quickly that no acrobat in the world save one who had learned it from the monkeys themselves could have done the trick. Tarzan himself trembled for a moment at the nearness of death to them.

As for the girl, her relief was so great that she could only cling to him and cry over and over again.

"Oh Tarzan! Oh, Tarzan. I knew Rokoff could never cover up his tracks so that you could not find him. I knew you would come to me!"

He tenderly held her close and smoothed her silky hair while he assured her over and over of his great and undying love for her.

"Sweetheart," he murmured. "I am doing my best to get you out of this jungle and to take you back to civilization where we may both be happy. Only be patient just a little longer and all our dreams will come true."

At length Tarzan drew away from the girl he loved and said, "Now, sweetheart, I must get you to my cabin before they can recapture you; then I must perform one act of justice both to myself and to the powers who sent me here. I am going to get Rokoff for keeps."

In vain Jane pleaded with him to think only of their own safety. Tarzan's anger was thoroughly aroused and he was determined to be avenged.

A little distance away on a small elevation the three conspirators, Sheik Ben Ali, Rokoff and Gernot had watched Tarzan swing downward from his high tree top to rescue Jane and they had also seen her tree fall.

Gernot was superstitiously inclined and

cried. "The ape man must command black magic! I saw him fall yet he is nowhere near the spot on which he should have landed, and her tree also has crashed to earth and she is no longer in it."

Ben Ali shrugged his lean shoulders and answered with a flash of his white teeth:

"Well, thank heaven he has his sweetheart. Now we can move against Opar in peace and get their gold!"

Rokoff whispered in an undertone to the Frenchman, "Ben Ali thinks we are through with Tarzan. If he knew Tarzan would trail us for the sheepskin he would turn back to the desert with his men."

The roaring of a lion near by sent them scurrying to safety and their conversation was not resumed until they had put a safe distance between themselves and the hungry animal.

Meantime Tarzan and Jane swung through the trees in safety as this was the quickest and most secret way they could reach the cabin by the sea. Tarzan held the girl in the hollow of his strong arm and swayed from branch to branch with a most unmortal-like security. One would have thought him some genius of the air—some spirit of magic, so sure was he on foot and of hand.

They had stopped in the hollow heart of an old tree to rest a bit when a sound came to them through the branches as of someone puffing and panting because he was out of breath. They looked down and what was their surprise and amusement to see Professor Porter, Jane's father, tricked out much in the same style as Tarzan, even to a lion skin thrown over his shoulder. He grasped in his pudgy hand a rudely cut stick on which he leaned his fat and puffy figure rather breathlessly, for it had been rough work ploughing his way through the tangled mass of creepers and thorns.

Professor Porter thought he had mastered the terrors of the jungle, but he had only done so in his own imagination.

Tarzan could not help laughing at the ridiculous mock heroic appearance he presented, and the professor, emitting what souned like a squeak of fear, hastily stretched his bow in their direction.

"Stop father! For Heaven's sake, don't shoot," cried Jane, fearing lest, in his clumsiness he really might hit them, and both she and Tarzan slipped down to the ground and were enfolded in the delighted professor's embrace.

"So," said Tarzan, slapping the little scientist on the back until he coughed, "You also have grown into a wild man."

"Oh, yes, indeed!" babbled Porter, glad to have an audience after all his lonely wanderings. "After all, my dear boy, it is quite easy and you see I am not afraid of nothing any more. I have indeed killed several lions. You see me wearing the skin of one of my victims."

Tarzan gave the lion's pelt a sharp look and then resumed gently: "Indeed, and how was that?"

The professor threw out his chest and drew a long breath. "Well, you see, my boy," he began, "this massive lion had me cornered in your cabin, and the actions of the dirty brute really got on my nerves so that I simply closed in with him as I have seen you do and stabbed him with my hunting knife after quite a desperate struggle. Several times indeed I thought he almost had me—"

The old liar was meditating on the

expediency of adding another lion to his tale to make it more thrilling, when Tarzan gently interrupted him by raising the end of the pelt and looking attentively at an inscription written on it in ink made from bark.

"My first lion," it read in Tarzan's unmistakable handwriting, and then followed a date at least several years old.

The professor gave it one shamefaced look and then good naturedly joined in the general laughter that followed.

"Well, I see that it is no use bluffing you young people," he chuckled.

"And now, dear," Tarzan interrupted somewhat gravely. "Your father's presence makes it possible for me to leave you in his care and take up the trail of Rokoff immediately. I shall join you both at my cabin."

Jane's lips quivered. "But Tarzan," she almost sobbed. "My dearest, they have guns!"

Tarzan drew himself up proudly. "And I have my strength and my agility which are more than a match for theirs," he answered. "Things are against them rather than me, dear."

But the winding trails of the forest had kept their enemies nearer to them than they thought. In a nearby thicket, Gernot and Rokoff had stopped to finish their plotting and planning.

Rokoff was frankly worried and made no attempt to conceal it. He knew that Tarzan was out for his life now as well as the parchment.

"Tarzan knows we are headed for Opar," he confided to Gernot. "I wish we could hide this parchment until we may return this way."

Gernot conceived a plan.

"We shall pass this water hole on our return from Opar," he suggested. "Why not conceal it here?"

"A great plan, my friend," approved the Russian, "and there is no time like the present!" Accordingly he allowed Gernot to hide the sheepskin behind some rocks and brush near the water hole, and the two friends walked away together from its hiding place and prepared to rejoin the others.

But all of a sudden there was a terrifying, singing, swishing sound through the air and Tarzan's trusty rope swung wickedly around Rokoff's burly figure, pinning his arms to his sides with its stinging touch. He had been lassoed by Jane's lover from the branch overhead. Rokoff's only answer was a roar of rage like that of a wounded animal as he vainly tried to free himself.

Gernot, jackal that he was, fled without making the slightest attempt to help him and when he was out of earshot he stopped and took counsel with himself. Then, after a moment's hesitation, he went straight to the cache near the water hole and stole the paper with which he had been entrusted.

Meanwhile Rokoff swung half choked in mid air while Tarzan shook him brutally and kept dinning into his ears a string of questions about the missing parchment.

"What have you done with it, you dog?" Tarzan cried, jerking the rope uncomfortably tight.

But Rokoff would only answer, "I've never seen the damned sheepskin since you took it from me at Hagar's."

"The truth isn't in you," Tarzan taunted back. "If what you say is true then who gassed me at the governor's house and took that sheepskin?"

And the denials of the Russian only brought

him fresh attentions with the rope.

Gernot, hiding the stolen parchment in his guilty bosom, ran into Ben Ali and the rest of the Arabs.

"Where is Rokoff?" demanded the sheik. "We cannot leave him behind. Turn back and search for him!"

Gernot was a little afraid of the tall, powerful Arab, and this was not at all what he wanted.

"Tarzan captured Rokoff and killed him," he lied, and Ben Ali plunged into the jungle in the direction where he had pointed, which was just opposite to the real one where Rokoff swung miserably from Tarzan's rope.

Then Gernot did something he had been longing to accomplish for some time. He crept along close to the base of the tree, unobserved by the two men, hastily snatching his revolver from his belt, he fired at his friend Rokoff with every intent to kill him, and fled as noiselessly as he came.

Unfortunately for Gernot's desires the bullet did not hit the Russian, it merely severed the rope and he had a nasty fall, from which he picked himself up barely able to walk, so great was the pain in his bruised ankles and legs.

The sound of shots nearby brought him out of the daze occasioned by his fall about as quickly as anything could and he limped off in their direction while Tarzan, also suspecting trouble, swung aloft in the trees.

He found that Ben Ali's men had captured the professor, who cried as he fell under their attack, "Run, Jane, and save yourself!"

The girl tried to do as she was told. She threw herself quite bravely into the thick

129

underbrush only to find herself straight in the path of some wild animal whose form she could make out half distinctly through the tree trunks.

With a shriek of terror, poor Jane doubled and turned back only to fall right into the enemy's hands.

"Some one is a traitor in this party," shouted Rokoff, his face black with rage as he came up with them. "I was shot from the branch of a tree."

"Yes, and you will be again!" answered Ben Ali as he aimed and discharged his revolver at an indistinct shape in the branches overhead. With an involuntary cry of pain Tarzan plunged down into their midst, shot in the same arm which he had with such difficulty healed only a short time before.

The Arabs fell upon him and mastered him after a sharp struggle which he gave them in spite of his helpless arm.

Rokoff fairly purred his pleasure and his cruel desire for revenge.

"And now, my fine friend, we shall make a real end of you," he gloated, "and possess our souls of peace. You shall be trussed up head downwards as a delicate feast for the lions which will soon be prowling around here for their evening meal."

Tarzan closed his eyes and tried not to conjure the picture.

Acting under the Russian's instructions, two of the Arabs climbed two small saplings and tied their top branches together. Then they fastened these to a rope and, to this swinging and revolving piece of hemp, they fastened head downward the helpless Tarzan, so securely trussed and tied he could not move an inch.

Then they retired to safety and left him to his fate. Slowly the sun neared its disappearing point below the horizon. Ominous night sounds began to fill the air; the shrill call of the water fowl, the scheech of sleepy parrots, the snarling, coughing roars of the big cats as they stretched themselves and arose to stalk their prey, and then came the pad of the lions' feet, the green glow of their eyes through the gloom.

Tarzan felt a hot breath against his ankle. Then there was a gentle exploring push of a great paw—then with a searing pain, like that of fire, the cruel thrust of claws, as the beast jumped up and caught him.

CHAPTER XIV

THE FLAMING ARROW

As Tarzan swung head downward from the rope to which he was tied hand and foot, the situation indeed looked desperate, and when the lion, sniffing at him in the darkness, stretched out his murderous claws and raked him with them, the pain was exquisite. But to the jungle bred Tarzan it was not so exquisite that he did not become conscious at the same time that the touch of those razor like claws had also severed the rope which bound his hands.

To think with Tarzan was invariably to act. He suffered none of the indecisions of men not bred to constant danger. His hands were free! No sooner did he realize this than, before the lion could do more than spring ineffectually at him, he had climbed hand over hand up the limb of a tree capable of supporting him. There he seated himself and unfastened the rest of the rope from his ankles, and when he was entirely free he could not resist giving a cry of defiance to the circle of gleaming eyes below.

He put compresses of healing leaves on his scratches during the night and slept cradled in the notch of a tree where there was no danger. In the morning he made his way through the tree tops thoroughly refreshed and full of courage.

With the first rays of the dawn Rokoff, Gernot and Ben Ali returned to where they had tied Tarzan. They expected to see very little of him left by the hungry lions. What was their surprise to find that he had escaped as attested by the rope which he had left behind him looped over the limb of a tree.

"He deals in black magic!" cried Ben Ali. "He is protected by the Djins whom Allah cursed. It is useless to fight against him. Let us go back to Sagarone before worse happens to us."

"And give up the gold of Opar? What folly!" Rokoff taunted. "Come, my superstitious friend, there is nothing supernatural about Tarzan. He was simply brought up in the wild and is more resourceful than we are and harder to kill, that is all. Come, courage! Soon the maidens and the gold of Opar will be ours!"

While Gernot was putting fresh heart into the sheik, Rokoff had quietly disappeared. He had felt vaquely uneasy about the parchment he had entrusted to the Frenchman and made his way to the water hole where he had hidden it. There he found his worst fears realized. Frantically pushing the leaves and branches aside in his haste, he found it had utterly disappeared.

Ben Ali and Gernot turned to speak to the Russian and guessed where he had gone. They looked at each other with significant glances.

"I wish we could get rid of him," the Frenchman remarked. "But he is the only one who knows the trail to Opar.

The wily Ben Ali frowned. "The girl knows the trail, she has been there," he suggested. "Let us capture her, and we can get rid of Rokoff after we have secured the gold."

They began to wrangle with some heat on the subject.

In the meantime, Tarzan, proceeding through the branches, heard a woman's scream and saw the professor and Jane being chased by a wild pig. The professor, far from being the hero he boasted when he told the lion story, ran just as hard as his daughter from the infuriated black and white sow whose litter they had disturbed. Smiling to himself, Tarzan sent his lariat whistling through the air and soon had the belligerent pig swinging and kicking in the air, a splendid breakfast for all three of them.

Professor Porter and Jane looked up at their deliverer and recognizing Tarzan, uttered cries of joy.

Jane flew to his arms and nestled there happily. "Oh, Tarzan dear," she cried, "We've had an awful time. First a great lion sprang from behind the bush where I was hiding and would have jumped upon me if it hadn't been for daddy. You needn't laugh; he was really brave. He shot the lion and rescued me just as you might have done."

The professor looked apologetically at Tarzan. "The funny part of it is that I don't know how I managed to hit him," he confessed honestly. "Of course, any father would do what he could to save his daughter, but then you know my laboratory work hasn't fitted me to be a particularly good shot—and well, I just aimed—and things happened, that's about all I know about it."

"And that's enough," commented Tarzan warmly. "Greater heroes than you, Porter, could not give any better explanation of their deeds. The main thing is that Jane is safe. And by the way, speaking of safety, how did you come to have that flesh wound in your arm?"

"One of the men, the Russian I think it was, took a shot at me as he saw me through the trees, and I think I did not run fast enough," said Jane's father. "Anyway, I must admit it hurts quite a lot and I feel a bit feverish. I wish there were some place where I might lie down and have a drink of water."

Tarzan examined the wound and bound it up afresh with leaves. "I am going to take you to my cabin. You can rest there and enjoy the freshness of the cool spring that flows near it. Then as it is near the sea, we can watch for the ship which the governor assured me would put in at the bay. I am going to send those two scoundrels back prisoners to France just as soon as I catch them. And when they reach France their term of life will be short."

In a short time Tarzan had led the professor to his cabin by the sea and made them comfortable. The professor stretched himself on the bunk of skins and Jane tenderly watched over him and put cold compresses on his wounded arm and feverish forehead.

The happiness of the three was disturbed, however, by strange noises from without. They were cries of rage from the ape tribe and Tarzan could in particular distinguish the voice of Naja raised in wrath as she violently flung cocoanuts and bad monkey language at some intruder. As the sounds grew in violence and threatened to become murderous, Tarzan thought it best to go out and investigate. He found the strange bull ape, Og, shuddering and endeavoring to make himself as small as possible in the midst of the mocking red-eyed group of apes who resented his presence, because they remembered what he had done to Tarzan the last time he was in their midst.

But Tarzan, much to Og's relief, stepped into the midst of the circle and raised his hand for silence.

"Shame on you, my brothers," said he, "that you tried to hurt this good ape who is now our faithful friend! See, he is trembling and bruised. From now on treat him as a brother, and you, Og, step forward and tell us what has brought you. I suppose it is a message from the people of Opar to whom I sent you."

"Yes, oh master," replied the ape. "Queen La sent me to ask you to lead her warriors to battle. She says she has no hope if you refuse to do this for the sake of your old friendship for her."

Tarzan thought a minute. "You mean," he said, "that Queen La wants me to lead her army in battle against Rokoff and Gernot and the Arabs?"

Og bowed his forehead in the dust. "Those were her wishes, O great Tarmangani," he replied.

Tarzan was about to answer when he was interrupted by a great cry, of what could be called nothing but jealousy, from the heretofore gentle Jane. Tarzan's eyes lighted with amusement as he saw her stamp her little foot, clench her rosy fists and tell Og what she thought of him for bringing such a dangerous proposition from the beautiful queen of Opar to her sweetheart.

"He shan't go! I won't let him be killed just as we are in sight of the ship which is to bear us to happiness and to France."

Tarzan put his hand over her angry red lips and held her closely but gently.

"Tell Queen La to defend herself against invasion," was his answer. "I will try to prevent the bandits from ever reaching Opar."

With this Og had to be content and he shambled back through the underbrush to bear his message.

Jane looked up at Tarzan with her eyes full

of tears. "Dearest, you would not, leave me!" she almost sobbed. "I am so afraid in that jungle."

Tarzan smiled down at her as he might at a child.

"I'm going to leave you and your father safely here for a little while," he said to her, "while I reconnoiter."

Gently releasing himself from Jane's arms he went out of the cabin and swung up into the trees. He moved swiftly and gracefully through their foliage until he heard the sound of voices and heard Gernot and Ben Ali in conversation. He came up in time to hear Gernot say:

"Porter escaped from your men. If he finds his daughter he is certain to head for Tarzan's cabin. That's where we will look for her."

"Well," returned Ben Ali, "I figure perhaps you are right and now I must go back and look after my bearers."

He disappeared into the jungle, and this gave Tarzan the very chance he was looking for. He hurled himself down from the trees and bore Gernot to the ground with the force of his impact. As the Frenchman lay there stunned and bleeding, Tarzan seized a stout stick, removed the cord from about his waist and passing the stick under his knees he fastened his wrists to it. He made a long end of the rope fast to the stick and throwing it over a stout limb he hoisted Gernot up into the branches.

The Frenchman threw him a glance of terror stricken appeal.

"Oh no, my friend," Tarzan answered him. "I shall not leave you to become lion bait. You are safe enough up there in the tree tops, but when I catch your master, Rokoff, you are both going to France my prisoners."

Gernot shuddered and closed his eyes. He knew what that meant. But Tarzan paid no attention to him and swung off again through the trees looking for Rokoff.

But as it happened he erred in his calculations. Rokoff was coming to the spot where Gernot was bound, from the opposite direction. The Russian's surprise at seeing his friend bound up in the tree overcame even his anger at discovering that Gernot had played him false and now held the formula in his possession instead of leaving it hidden near the water hole. This was Tarzan's work, and it reminded him only too well that they both stood in mortal danger from him, and that this was no time for squabbling.

Rokoff, therefore, cut the rope which held Gernot high up in the tree and when he had lowered him he untied the ropes and chafed his wrists.

Gernot, the moment he had recovered his breath, began to whimper an explanation. "Tarzan has your formula and map. He left me prisoner and he is now looking for you."

Rokoff swore. "That ape man still alive? Damn him!"

Gernot sighed. "Yes, and more than that," he added, "he must be expecting a ship, for he swore he would take you and me back to France."

"Let us go to the cabin and capture his sweetheart and get revenge on him in that way, then we'll go on to Opar and capture the city. I am positive I can find my way to the treasure vault."

The two rascals made their way through the jungle in the direction of Tarzan's cabin. When it came into view they hid in the bushes and waited to get some information if possible. They could see the dim outline of a man moving around, and then the door opened and Jane came out with a pitcher. She wanted to get water at the spring. Rokoff nudged Gernot and prepared to rush forward and seize her when, with a shriek of fright, Jane dashed back into the cabin and slammed the door just in time to avoid the rush and spring of a great black maned lion.

Rokoff drew his revolver and shot the beast. Jane, hearing the shot, looked out of the narrow window and saw his evil face over the smoking gunbarrel.

"Rokoff!" she cried to her father in terror and hid her face in her trembling hands.

The Russian's feelings underwent one of those swift changes only the Slav disposition is capable. His face grew black with hate.

"I believe it is Tarzan who is in there with her!" he said to Gernot. "Let us burn them in the cabin like rats in a trap."

He reached for a small fire bomb in his knapsack and hurled in against the flimsy woodwork of the cabin. It exploded with a great burst of flame and in a minute the entire structure was a mass of fire.

Jane and the wounded professor inside wildly tried to escape. The flames cut them off in every direction. The professor sank on his couch helplessly. Jane fell unconscious on the blazing floor.

CHAPTER XV

THE LAST ADVENTURE

"We'll burn them both like rats in the cabin," the revengeful Rokoff exclaimed, when he threw the fire bomb which set fire to Tarzan's cabin, for he thought in his jealous rage the lovers were inside.

But it was only Jane and her wounded father whom they trapped. Tarzan, from his vantage point high up in the trees, smelled the smoke and turning in the right direction saw the glare of his burning hut. Pale with terror at the danger he knew his sweetheart was in, he fairly flew from branch to branch to her rescue. Finally, after what seemed ages but was only a few seconds, he dropped from the nearest tree and burst into the blazing doorway.

He saw the professor unconscious from the smoke, on the bunk and Jane lying face downward on the floor with the flames creeping toward the edge of her skirt. Holding his breath lest he swallow any of the deadly flames, Tarzan lifted up a trap door in the flooring and seizing Jane, he dropped her gently down into the cellar storehouse, after which he went back and did the same to the professor, then he lowered himself through the entrance and the three of them reached the little earthern tunnel which led from the cellar.

As they watched the flames die down after having destroyed Tarzan's home, he pointed in the distance where the discomfitted Rokoff, Gernot and Ben Ali moved on with their Arab train of bandits in the direction of Opar.

"Dearest," he said. "You are safe now, they will not return for greed has them in its clutches. The callar is safe if any wild beast attempts to attack you. I must reconnoiter." He meant that he must go to the rescue of Queen La, but he took this method of allaying her jealousy.

He swung himself up into the branches and was out of sight before she could answer his last kiss and his whispered words of love. Much as he hated to leave the girl he loved, Tarzan felt that honor demanded that he go to the help of the unfortunate Queen of Opar and her dwarfs who were about to lose all they had in the world, through the treachery of white men like himself.

He had not proceeded far when he heard cries and shrieks of rage from some big ape, who was evidently being manhandled and, looking down through the branches, he saw the unfortunate Og in the hands of the band of thieves. With threats and with blows they tried to force him to lead them through the shortest and safest route into Opar. Og refused valiantly until the cruel Ben Ali drew his two-edged dagger and advanced toward him.

"Dog of an accursed evil spirit, for thou knowest more than were beast should, use thy knowledge to lead the followers of the true faith where they may find maidens and treasure or else death is at thy throat!" He pressed the keen-edged dagger at the hairy throat of poor Og and the ape, with a shriek of terror, signified by groans and convulsive movements of his whole body that he would do whatever they wished. He shambled off, in the lead, along the road which led to Opar and which showed by its rocky character that they were drawing near to the hidden city.

Tarzan followed as best he could by leaping from branch to branch and he arrived in time to see the vanguard of the dwarfs attempt to defend their stronghold. They had none of the weapons of modern warfare, of course, and they tried to check the advance of the Arab robbers by rolling down upon them huge boulders from the rocky passes above.

But the Arabs were too clever for them and too quick. They managed to evade most of the rocks. After one or two almost useless attempts to crush their enemies, after they had seen their boulders, which it took the strength of many to lift, roll harmlessly down the mountainside, the dwarfs retreated in despair. Perhaps it should be said that they attempted to retreat, for the Arabs immediately opened fire and the uncomfortable little brown men were mowed down until such as escaped ran wildly in the utmost confusion.

Tarzan saw that something must be done to save Opar and that quickly or it would be too late. He remembered the crevice in the mountainside through which he had fallen the last time he was there when the earthquake occurred. He dropped from his tree and doubling on his tracks, circled around in the opposite direction and sought the short cut up the steep side of the mountain which he knew so well. As he reached the crevice and prepared to leap down into its depths, the sounds of battle reached him, proving that he was all but too late, and indeed the battle between the Arabs and Queen La's warriors was raging fast and furious in the very midst of the temple of sacrifice.

La, the queen, pale and majestic, in all her trappings of high priestess, stood in the treasure chamber surrounded by her shrieking and terror stricken hand-maidens. The queen seemed as if paralyzed by the enormity of her misfortunes. In desperation she had released the lions. There was nothing left that she could do, but with lips that uttered no sounds she prayed to her gods.

It seemed a direct answer that all at once Tarzan stood before her. At first she thought that she of died of her sorrow and despair and that he was a spirit, and then she realized where she was and that he was indeed a living and breathing man. The wonderful thought came to her that he had come to save her because he loved her.

"My king!" she cried, and threw self on his breast.

But Tarzan gently released her. "No, La," he answered her. "Not your king, but your friend, who will help you keep what is yours and rid you of your enemies."

The queen bowed her head in despair. "They are even now quarreling over the the treasure in the temple of sacrifice; in a few moments they will burst into this vault and kill us all," she moaned.

Tarzan took from the folds of his leopard skin a package of powder tied in a skin.

"Build a fire in the tunnel which leads from the temple of sacrifice to this room and scatter handfuls of this powder on it," he commanded. "It will stupefy them and I will roll back the rock over them from the outside."

With hope springing anew in her breast, the queen ordered his commands to be obeyed. Even the maidens helped the warriors pile up all the inflammable maternal they could could put their hands upon and set fire to it, after they had first scattered over it thoroughly the powder Tarzan had given them.

When the Arabs, led by Ben Ali and Rokoff,

dashed into the tunnel, they were met by a thick, yellowish smoke which they attempted to fight for about only one minute before they sank unconscious to the ground where they lay like the very dead. As the smoke reached every corner of the cavern the others sank under its influence one by one in spite of their efforts to find the entrance which Tarzan from the outside had carefully blocked.

When he decided the smoke had time to produce its effect, Tarzan rolled the stone to one side and jumped into the cave. The sight which met his eyes was a strange one. The air that Tarzan let in enabled him to enter with impunity and he quickly went from man to man, binding them while they were still unconscious, with the help of the dwarfs. When he came to Gernot and Rokoff he took the great rope from around his neck and tied it to them as if they were cattle about to be driven to market.

After he had them securely tied, he left them for a moment and went to the side of La, where she stood surrounded by her warriors.

"You are safe, O Queen," he cried. "Beware how you trust strangers another time, for I may not be near to save you." He stretched out his hand to her.

"Stay, oh stay," she implored him.

"That is impossible, even if I would, for I must take the ship which probably waits for me in the bay and take these scoundrels prisoners to France."

"And the little brown-haired maiden with the white skin goes with you—?" La's voice was husky with her despair.

"She goes with me—for all time."

The queen's tawny head drooped in her

sorrow. She knew she had lost this man forever.

"Good-bye, La." Tarzan turned on his heel and was gone.

She stretched out her arms heavy with their barbaric bracelets as if by that gesture and the agony in her heart she might call him back—but he was gone out of her life and she sank back into the arms of her women with the sorrow of it.

In the meantime, Tarzan had seized the end of the rope which held bound together his two captives and had forced them by dragging them when they would not move otherwise, to go through the narrow opening and down the mountain side. With curses and wild threats, Rokoff and Gernot tried to resist, only to be dragged, half choked, over rocks and down ravines, until finally by the time they came in sight off the sea the captives were quiet and walked with the docility of despair.

There was a great surprise ready for Tarzan when he reached the ocean, for Jane, knowing his plans had decided she could not wait for him any longer, and she and her father had left the cabin and proceeded through the short distance of jungle which separted it from the shore.

On the way they had a narrow escape from a lion which forced her to take refuge in a tree until the professor came up and bravely frightened the animal by stoning it.

"When we reach the shore we must build signal fires," said Jane, as she lifted her head from her father's arms. "Then, if Tarzan returns, as he said he would, we must take that ship he is waiting for and leave this jungle for ever."

"Yes, indeed, my girl," answered her father. "A great and glorious future awaits Tarzan in the lands of civilization where I know he will be willing to stay for your sake, now he has won your love."

And so, as Tarzan reached the beach with his captives he saw in the growing dusk the glow of fires on the smooth expanse of whie sand, and, in answer to his shout and his upflung arms, a little figure came running toward him.

"My dearest and my darling," cried Tarzan. "Our troubles are over. Soon the French ship will be here and we shall be on our way toward calmer, happier lands."

There was a harsh cry filled with grief and pathetic appeal and a shaggy ape bounded across the sands at Tarzan's feet. He bent over the and patted the rough, homely head.

"Have they driven you away, my poor Og?" he said. "Then you shall come with us. You could not help what you did, there were too many for you and I forgive you."

Tarzan took Og and Professor Porter back to the little clump of trees where he had left his prisoners.

"Guard them for me," he said to Porter and Og; and while the latter growled his fierceness the professor looked at the pair with no less determination over the top of a very wicked looking gun barrel.

Tarzan filled a gourd with water and offered it to the men. Rokoff drank eagerly. Gernot turned away with hatred shining from his evil eyes.

"Gentlemen, you had better resign yourselves," warned Tarzan, "for at any moment the cutter will arrive to take us to the ship which will bear you prisoners to France."

Gernot sneered. "—and Ben Ali—he escapes your vengeance?"

Tarzan became very grave. "Mine perhaps," he answered. "But not that of fate, for as I left the cavern I saw one of the lions La freed from the treasure vault spring on his body and tear his throat. Ben Ali has already gone to pay his account."

He placed his arm around Jane and gently drew her away toward the shore, but first they passed through the little thicket which encircled the spring. There was the pad of furry feet and Jane drew closer to Tarzan but he smiled at her fears.

"They will not hurt us, they have come for water—watch them for the last time—our jungle friends," he said gently.

First a couple of young leopards came frisking in the light of the rising moon and drank daintily without wetting their wonderful coats of spotted velvet. Then a wild hog ran around in circles, barked once shrilly to its mate and lapped noisily at the gurgling stream. Last of all, a kingly lion, with a black mane and a majestic stride, lowered his royal head and drank from where the spring splashed coolest in its depths.

After he had left, the branches overhead became alive with chattering apes.

"Good-bye, my brothers," said Tarzan and his voice was a little husky with emotion.

In the distance there was a great crashing of branches and of bushes as at the passage of some huge animal. Tarzan laughed aloud and threw up his arm.

"Tantor," he cried, in the old remembered way.

Through the stillness of the forest came the trumpeting answer.

"Dear Tantor!" Jane murmured gently, as she smiled up at her tall lover.

They walked to the beach where the sands now shone like silver in the splendid light of the tropical moon. Clasped in each other's arms they watched for the ship to appear and the moon made a bright path across the water like a radiant finger beckoning them to happiness. It was so bright and they were so wrapped in each and weaving their dreams about it that they did not notice the approach of the ship until it came directly into the path of the light and they saw the boat lowered and rapidly approaching the shore.

"The ship!" cried Jane, who saw it first. "Thank God, we are saved!"

"Yes, dear," Tarzan answered tenderly. "The ship which is to bring us happiness."

Did you enjoy this book on the 15 Chapter Serial, *Adventures of Tarzan*? Interested in finding out more about this serial as well as the rest of the Tarzan series? Be sure to buy your copies of the **EDGAR RICE BURROUGHS AND THE SILVER SCREEN** series researched and written by Jerry L. Schneider.

Now available:

Book 1 — 1917-1919
Book 2 — 1920-1929
Book 3 — 1930-1939
Book 4 — 1940-1949
Book 5 — 1950-1959
and
Tarzan MGM Pictorial

Available at

www.FictionHousePress.com

www.ingramcontent.com/pod-product-compliance
Lightning Source LLC
Chambersburg PA
CBHW060403030726
47497CB00003B/834